INDECENT
EXPOSURE

INDECENT EXPOSURE

AC ARTHUR

www.urbanbooks.net

Urban Books
1199 Straight Path
West Babylon, NY 11704

ISBN- 13: 978-1-60162-177-1
ISBN- 10: 1-60162-177-9

First Printing July 2009
Printed in the United States of America

10   9   8   7   6   5   4   3   2   1

*This is a work of fiction. Any references or similarities to actual
events, real people, living, or dead, or to real locales are intended to give the novel a sense of reality. Any similarity in other
names, characters, places, and incidents is entirely coinciden-
tal.*

Distributed by Kensington Publishing Corp.
Submit Wholesale Orders to:
Kensington Publishing Corp.
C/O Penguin Group (USA) Inc.
Attention: Order Processing
405 Murray Hill Parkway
East Rutherford, NJ 07073-2316
Phone: 1-800-526-0275
Fax: 1-800-227-9604

Acknowledgments

To all the members of AC Arthur's Book Lounge, thanks so much for your constant encouragement and support, you made this book a reality.

Thanks to Family Matters for your love and support.

As always I thank Damon and the kids for giving up wifey and mommy several hours each day, allowing me the time to get lost in the writing world. I know it's not always easy and I sincerely appreciate your sacrifice.

INDECENT
EXPOSURE

Chapter 1

N *ow let's find the no-good, cheating asshole*, Nola
Brentwood thought to herself as she stepped off the
elevator into the posh reception area of Censor Creative
Media.

Decorated in a rich burgundy hue and plush gray car-
pets, from the crown molding on the walls to the brass
handles on the glass doors, Censor's home office spoke
volumes to their success. By way of research for this assignment Nola now knew that Censor had been family
owned and run for the last twenty-five years, but had
only reached the top of the advertising game in the last
ten. This office, however, was fairly new, occupying space
in downtown Baltimore's newest skyscraper.

This was Nola's fifth assignment in the ten months
since her private investigation office had opened. Breakdown, as she'd so aptly named her company, was designed for the woman not only looking to catch her man
cheating, but for the woman who was determined to get
even.

After her six-month stay in jail for assault, Nola still

hadn't gotten over the sting of betrayal at the hands of her cousin, Jenna and her trifling-ass boyfriend, Mark. No, correct that, she had gotten over that. What she hadn't and probably would never get over was the gall of some men to do the low-down, disgusting things they did to women. Moreover, she was determined to never let them get away with it again.

Almost two years ago Nola had met Mark Riley, or the man she knew as Mark Riley. He was a law clerk in the firm where she was a partner. As a result of her two closest friends and cousins, Serena and Cally, coming up with the idiotic plan that they would all take dates to their hometown of St. Michaels, Maryland where their cousin, Jenna, was getting married, Nola had broken one of her hard and steadfast rules. Never before had she even considered dating a man she worked with, and a man that was in a position beneath her at that. Still, desperate times had called for desperate measures. To keep their mothers from harping on the fact that they didn't have men of their own, Cally, Serena, and Nola had quickly found weekend dates.

For Nola, Mark had turned out to be a weekend mistake. After a week in his bed and to everyone's shock and dismay Mark Riley turned out to be Mark Drew Riley, Jenna's ex-boyfriend. That fact had been revealed while they all partied with Jenna and her fiancé during the rehearsal dinner, proving to Nola once again that men were no damned good.

Unfortunately, Jenna, in Nola's opinion, was just as stupid and conniving as Mark or Drew or whoever, because she took him back, leaving her rich and influential husband-to-be-looking like a fool. But Nola wasn't gullible and she wasn't above getting revenge. Shooting Mark had been all about revenge. Fortunately for Nola, her lack of a prior record and the excellent high-priced lawyer she'd retained got her off with three years jail time, all but six months suspended.

So Breakdown was funded and opened with her own idea and her own money. Sure, Cally and Serena had helped her, once they'd gotten past the revenge-for-hire theme to the business, of course. Cally and Serena had found happiness with the men of their choices. Serena had married James, her high school sweetheart, while Cally and Steven were still happily living together. And Nola certainly did not begrudge them their good fortune. She just didn't believe in fairy tales. She lived in the real world, the one where her bastard of a father had left her mother with an infant and never looked back.

Nola's thought behind the company was to catch cheating men, husbands or boyfriends and break them down completely. Attack their careers, their personal con- nections—any and everything until they saw the error of their ways and begged for mercy or gave their women significant monetary settlements that would make up for the hurt and misery they'd put them through, whichever came first.

It was lucrative, to say the least. So far Nola had helped wives of politicians, girlfriends of professional sports players and housewives of CEOs. Her bank account was heftier now than it had been when she'd been fired from her job at the law firm for shooting fool-ass Mark in the balls.

This was her calling.

"May I help you, ma'am?"

Nola's attention snapped to the woman sitting behind the marble desk. She was pretty enough, with her per- fectly tanned skin and amber eyes. Her hair was cut in a stylish bob a few inches longer than Nola's own, short crop. Her lips were full, covered in a peach gloss. . . . Nola caught herself mid-thought. Ever since Serena had shared her threesome experience with Cally and Nola, Nola had been seeing women in a different light.

It was probably natural since she practically hated all men, that Nola finally tried her own hand at a female-female encounter. She remembered Kandy and her dark, smooth skin, the way she'd rubbed her naked body all along Nola's butter-toned one. That night had been a wonderful experience, one Nola was sure she'd indulge in again. But not right now and not with this smiling receptionist.

Today was strictly about business.

"I apologize," she began with her own smooth smile. "I'm here for the Panzene meeting. I think I might be a few minutes late."

The girl nodded her head, then stood and came around the desk. "Yes, they started about fifteen minutes ago. I'll show you which conference room they're in."

"Thank you," Nola said, smiling, and fell into step behind the woman, enjoying the view as she walked.

The Panzene meeting was with the advertising group and the key players at the Panzene Corporation, an exotic cosmetics company. Lisette Williamson, Nola's client, had given her the complete rundown of Panzene and the large account that CCM had fought long and hard to obtain. Now that CCM and its top group of advertising executives had pulled off the coup of the century by snagging this exclusive deal with Panzene, they had no choice but to wow them. Shooting their first round of commercials at the Horizon, Antigua's beautiful hedonistic resort, was an impressive step in that direction.

Nola was allowed into the meeting through Lisette's connections to both boards of directors at Panzene and at CCM. Her sole purpose was to find out which woman in the company Bernard Williamson, Lisette's husband, was sleeping with. Nola didn't know specifically how Lisette was connected to the board of directors for both companies and didn't really care to. If it didn't directly involve her assignment, she simply brushed it aside.

The pretty receptionist opened the door for her and Nola offered her a smile before entering the room full of—at a quick glance—four men and two women.

"Good morning," she said. "Sorry I'm late. I'm—"

"You're Kingsley Mason from Panzene's Toronto office."

Answering to the name she'd taken for the purpose of this assignment, Nola's gaze shifted quickly to the tall, dark-skinned man who had stood and now walked toward her with his hand extended.

"Yes, I am," she replied, not the least bit impressed by his height or his well-fitting suit. Men were so cocky, always thinking that all they had to do was stand up in front of a woman to impress her. Because this was business, Nola shook his hand and assumed the identity she and her client had worked out.

This would put Nola right in the middle of this campaign, in range of Bernard Williamson and the woman she suspected him of sleeping with. Lisette didn't have a name for the woman, only that they were working on this project closely. So with only two other females in the room Nola didn't anticipate having a difficult time figuring this out. Lisette was certain that the woman her husband was sleeping with was working on this Panzene account with him. Thus the field had been narrowed for Nola before she'd even arrived.

"I'm Leonard Black, senior account exec for Censor. It's a pleasure to meet you."

Why was it a pleasure? Nola thought. *Because I'm wearing this low-cut camisole and tight-fitting suit, most likely.* Look at him, he was already eyeing her like she was the main course at a barbeque. "The pleasure is all mine, Mr. Black. Now where do I sit so we can continue?"

Mr. Black, wearing cologne that Nola recognized as Burberry Touch and with a ready smile, led her to a seat that was, surprise, right next to his own. When she was seated he took the liberty of making introductions. "From the top, this is Corbin Censor, our CEO and Jerome Petti-way, junior account exec."

Nola was amazed at how he'd stressed "junior," meaning the other man was below him. She hid her laughter at this fool only because she needed to focus on putting names with faces.

"This is Casey McKnight," Leonard continued. "She's an account exec and this is Meosha Cannon, assistant copywriter. Bernard Williamson is the vice president and management supervisor here at CCM."

He kept talking and while Nola's gaze went to each person introduced to her, her mind had paused at Bernard Williamson.

He was what one would call a fine-ass brother. His skin was buttery smooth, just a shade darker than her own. His close-cropped hair was cut precisely, his face clean-shaven, with thick eyebrows and bedroom dark brown eyes. Even through the outline of his suit Nola could tell he was buff. The gold cuff links and wristwatch said he took his appearance seriously. The way his gaze had roamed over her for a second more than was profes-sional said he was just as his wife had predicted—a lying, cheating bastard of the lowest form.

"Shall we continue?" she asked, knowing she really didn't care what they did at this meeting. Her sole pur-pose here was to observe.

Was it the too cute Casey McKnight, with her long curly black hair and perky smile? Or was it Meosha Cannon,

the mocha-toned beauty with sensually slanted eyes, giving her an Asian flare?

Bernard was sleeping with one of these women and
she was going to find out which one, then make his ass
pay!

That meeting had been long, then Nola had to endure
lunch with the very astute Leonard Black. Luckily, Bernard thought it was wise that he participate in the
schmoozing of their biggest client, so he'd joined them.
Two hours of Nola's afternoon were spent between two
very attractive, very intriguing men, who had taken flirta-
tion to a new level. Though neither of them did anything
overt, beyond the eye contact and double entendres,
Nola knew that if she simply asked they'd be at her
condo, naked and in her bed. Such a damned pity.

Putting the key into her door and dropping her briefcase, Nola breathed a sigh of relief that her work for
today was over. Now all she wanted to do was take a
much-needed nap.

But when she waltzed into her bedroom and found a
man lying across her bed, naked as the day he was born,
Nola knew she wouldn't be going to sleep for a while.
Even with her biased view of the opposite sex, thanks to
her no-good father, this was one man she welcomed in
her bed whenever he appeared.

"It's about time you got home," he said with that slow,
purposeful drawl of his.

Nola couldn't get enough of this man. No matter how
she felt about the species as a whole, Sgt. Gerard "Gee"
Matthews had some kind of whip appeal on her.

If she hadn't met him in the jail she would have sworn
he was a bodybuilder. Even now his caramel-toned skin
glistened, the thick, well-honed muscles rippling and
bulging, a true testament to his many hours spent at the

gym. Was it his bald head or his tattooed arms that turned her on more? Nola considered this as she unbuttoned her blouse. "Were you waiting for me long?" she asked coyly, knowing he could have been here anywhere from one to the five and a half hours she'd been away from home. He had a key to her condo, which for Nola had been her one moment of weakness with Gee. She did not do live-in boyfriends. Her house was her own space and when she was ready for a man to leave she had no problem kicking him out. Why she'd given Gee a key was still a mystery to her. One she wasn't up to figuring out right now.

He shifted so that his legs were spread just a bit wider, clasping his hands behind his head that was already propped up on pillows. "Long enough," he replied. "Hurry up and bring that ass over here."

And just like that she was wet. In addition to the thick muscles and ribbed abs, Gee had a delicious dick that never failed to bring Nola pleasure. From the first night he'd pressed her face against the cool cement wall in her cell and rammed his thick length past her ass into her pussy, she'd been a slave to his cock and she wasn't ashamed to admit it.

Even Kandy and her magnificent tongue hadn't been able to erase Gee from Nola's mind.

Her clothes now lay in a heap on the floor as she climbed up onto her four-poster bed. Gee didn't move a muscle. He simply waited for her to do as he said. But no matter how dick-whipped he had her, Nola didn't oblige too easily. Dragging her hands along his calves and up his meaty thighs, she looked down at the object of her desire. God, she loved the look of his dick, hard and ready for her.

Grasping him roughly at the base she immediately

flicked her tongue over its bulbous head. Again, Gee remained still. Determined to get a rise—another rise—out of him, Nola took his entire length into her mouth. Normally she toyed with him, licking up and down the long shaft, toying with his balls while jerking him off. Today she simply went for the gusto.

He hit the base of her throat and she hummed, tightened her jaws and sucked upward. After repeating this motion twice, her hand wet from the saliva her mouth produced around his length, she smiled when finally one of his large hands went to the base of her head.

"Nobody sucks cock like you, baby," he groaned and applied pressure to her head, pushing her down again.

Nola and Gee had an open relationship, which meant they were both free to see and sleep with other people. There was no commitment with them, no obligations or responsibilities. She insisted on that when she'd been released from the jail where she'd first met her correctional officer lover. A few weeks prior to her release, Gee had begun talking about them moving in together. Nola had quickly nipped that in the bud. She and Gee were lovers, plain and simple, and they weren't exclusive. That's not what she wanted in her life. And if Gee wanted to continue fucking her—which she knew he did—he would abide by her rules.

She continued to work her mouth over him until her thighs were quivering, her pussy dripping with need. She released his cock from her mouth with a plopping sound and said, "Are you just going to lay there or what?"

He smiled, that crooked grin that he gave when he was about to tear into her ass. Her heart leapt as she scooted off the bed. Her favorite position with Gee—and maybe this was because it was the position they'd assumed the six months she was locked up—was from the back.

She stood at the side of the bed and bent forward, being sure to grasp handfuls of the comforter in her fingers. With Gee it was best to hold on.

He'd gotten up off the bed, found a condom, ripped the package, and smoothed it on. Then he'd approached her from behind with a resounding slap to her ass. She didn't scream; they'd been well-versed in being as quiet as possible in the jail as well. Gee didn't want to share her with his coworkers, nor did he want to get fired. Nola just wanted to do her time and move on.

"You ready for me, baby?"

"Oh yeah," Nola replied, lowering herself to the mattress so that her puckered nipples could receive some stimulation.

Her motion was immediately paused by another smack to her ass. "You know better than that. I'll touch them when I'm ready," Gee growled from behind.

Nola instantly lifted from the bed, holding firm in her position. Gee liked her ass in the air and her tits swaying. He did not allow her to bring herself release in any way, shape or form. That's what he was there for.

So with one hand he thrust three fingers into her waiting pussy while wrapping the other around her torso to grab her left tit. Squeezing and pumping simultaneously, Nola had to bite her bottom lip to keep from screaming out.

"Yeah, you're ready," he said and she could tell that he was grinning. He pulled his fingers out of her and Nola knew he'd put them in his mouth. The low moan coming from him a second later proved her point.

"Did you think about me today, Nola?" Gee asked as he positioned his dick at her entrance.

She could lie, but what would be the point? "No," she replied then sucked in a breath when he held still, the tip just barely knocking at pleasure's door.

Cursing, Nola looked over her shoulder at him. "Are we doing this or not?"

"I'm asking the questions," he said, grabbing hold of his swollen cock and moving it up and down her juiciness. "I thought about you. All last night and the first thing this morning. I thought about you. That's why I came over here but you were already gone."

While he talked, Gee teased her, scraping his arousal over her tightened clit, pushing inside her center a half an inch, then pulling back out.

"I've been laying here for hours thinking of how much I wanted to fuck and suck you."

Nola wiggled her ass and moaned. If that's what he'd been thinking about then he needed to come on and do it.

"Now I want to know if you thought about me too."

"I said no!" Nola yelled, then moved out of his reach to sit on the bed. "Why do we have to keep going over this, Gee? Why can't we just be like we were before?"

"Because you're no longer locked up and because I want to be more than just your fuck buddy."

Nola looked up at him, this magnificently built specimen who stood not even a foot away from her holding his thick cock in one hand while rubbing his bald head with the other. "I can't give you more than that."

"Can't or won't, Nola?"

"We've been all through this before," she said, standing up and pushing past him to get to her closet where she could retrieve her robe. If she wasn't getting any there was no point in traipsing around naked. "Either-or. Take your pick. That's just the way it is," she said without turning to look at him.

That had been a mistake. Gee was a very physical man, most likely because he worked in a locked prison with hardened criminals on a daily basis. At any rate, Nola had learned, from the way he dealt with other inmates while she'd been in jail, that his physical nature could go to much greater heights than she'd ever personally experienced.

The second she felt his hands wrap around her arms she knew she was about to get a glimpse of it in person. Gee lifted her from the floor and tossed her back onto the bed. She bounced at first contact then tried to right herself. "What the hell are you doing?"

"Shut up!" he roared, then lifted her legs, dropping them onto his massive shoulders and entering her in one fast thrust.

"Gee," she gasped as he pulled out of her, then slammed back into her with such force she moved upward a few inches on the bed.

"All I want to hear is how good it is to you, Nola," he said through clenched teeth and pulled out of her again. "Just tell me it's good." Sinking back inside of her, he waited expectantly.

Nola closed her eyes. There were some things in life she just couldn't deny. The fact that her father was an asshole was one and the fact that Sgt. Gee Matthews was an excellent lover was another.

"It's good, baby," she whispered, reaching her arms up to touch his tattooed chest. "It's so damn good."

Chapter 2

Lisette Williamson's mother was visiting this week so Bernard made a point of staying at the office as long as he possibly could.

Doing so had two advantages: one, he could avoid the evil eye his mother-in-law always gave him and the third degree she would give Lisette about how he was treating her; and two, he could spend even more time watching the woman he really wanted.

Casey McKnight was an account executive at CCM, overseeing some of the smaller accounts the company had by analyzing competitive activity and consumer trends. She'd been with the firm for a little over two years and in that time had impressed the higher brass. More certainly, she'd impressed Bernard.

Being a senior vice president with a foot and a half in the door to becoming president, then answering only to Corbin Censor, the CEO, Bernard had the privilege of hiring new account execs as well as supervising their growth and the growth of their accounts. He'd never loved his job more than the day Casey had interviewed with him.

She was pretty in an innocent way that had immediately captured him. A review of her job application told him she was three years out of college with a bachelor's degree in marketing and advertising and that she was twenty-five years old, making him older than her by eight years. Her quick wit and intelligence only earned her more brownie points. And when she'd stood to leave, the perfection of each of her womanly curves had sealed the deal. Not only was he intent on hiring her, he was determined to fuck her.

For the first few months his fascination with Casey had been purely physical. But as they'd worked closely on a couple of accounts he'd grown to like her on a personal level. But alas, that closeness had proved a hindrance. One night, about four months after they'd been working really late, Bernard had convinced Casey that they should grab some dinner before going home. That's when he'd found out she had a boyfriend. A live-in boyfriend at that.

His name was Simon. Who the hell named their son, a black man, Simon? Better yet, what was Simon doing for Casey that he couldn't? For starters, Simon wasn't married. That was always the first answer to that question.

Bernard was a married man, starving for another man's woman. Wasn't that a kick in the ass?

No, being married to Lisette was. They'd met in college while he was studying for his master's and she her bachelor's degree and had hit it off instantly. The sex was hot and she was great company at parties, but that was it. Bernard hadn't once thought about a future with the Delta chick that had come to his dorm room naked on a dare one winter night.

But on the eve of his graduation, when she'd come to him and announced that she was pregnant, that future had been quickly forced upon him. They were married the month after he graduated and a week later he started his internship at CCM. That had been seven years ago.

Madison, his six-year-old daughter, was the best and most beautiful thing to come out of that union. Now he and Lisette simply coexisted. They were married on paper, on the mortgage to their Columbia, Maryland home and the BMW he drove and Lexus she used, but beyond that, there was nothing. At least on his part wasn't.

The affairs had started the month after Madison was born. Bernard didn't even remember the first woman's name. He'd taken her in the backseat of his car after a business meeting. From that point on, he'd found his one and only outlet to his doomed marriage. There wasn't a day that didn't go by that Bernard didn't think of picking up that phone and calling his attorney, Rex Bateman, letting him know he wanted to file for divorce.

What was stopping him? Madison, for one. He'd grown up in a stable home with both parents. Whether or not he knew for sure his parents were happy the duration of their marriage, Bernard had no idea. All he knew was that he'd felt privileged as a black male with both his mother and father living in the house with him. He wanted Madison to have that same privilege.

Another contributing factor would be that Lisette's father, Arnold Winston, was very influential in the city of Baltimore. So much so that the mayor consulted with him on decisions, too many businesses to count asked him to be on their boards, and his name was always being mentioned in the newspapers. Arnold Winston was a force to be reckoned with and right now he had plans to seat his son-in-law on the city council. Bernard was a little on the fence about politics but Arnold was a very persuasive man.

So Bernard stayed with Lisette, but he didn't love her. He never had. He'd simply had sex with her, gotten her pregnant, and felt duty-bound to marry her.

Then again, what couple fell in love and stayed in love these days? He'd seen so many relationships crash and burn that he felt he and Lisette were doing the honorable thing. He doubted Lisette had any more feelings for him than he did her. Did she have affairs as well? Bernard didn't know and didn't care to find out. It was definitely true that a man was cool with his own marital indiscretions, but the thought of his wife stepping out was cause for murderous thoughts he wasn't in the mood to entertain.

What he had entertained and was thinking that it was finally time to move on from, was the newly promoted copywriter. Meosha Cannon. She'd been an administrative assistant in human resources when Bernard had first met her. One look at that plump, round ass in that tight skirt she'd been wearing and he knew he had to have a piece.

Two weeks later he and Meosha shared a very memorable liaison in the stairwell near the garage exit. From that moment on it had been nonstop with her. She was insatiable, which turned him on to no end. But she was also ambitious and borderline greedy. That could pose a problem, because he wasn't prepared to do any more for her than he already had. A menial promotion from administrative assistant to copywriter was all he was going to do for Meosha by way of employment. Bernard figured if she could proofread the daily correspondence that went out, she could proofread the text to their ads and proposals just as well. Anything beyond that would be out of Meosha's realm, in his opinion. Now she was on the team that brought Panzene to CCM. She would also be going on the trip to Antigua to shoot the commercial.

Bernard knew he needed to break things off with Meosha before they left on Friday. Casey would also be going on the trip and he fully intended to take this opportunity to sweep the beautiful Ms. McKnight off her feet.

With that in mind he'd called Meosha and asked her to come to his office once he'd returned from lunch with Leonard and the Panzene rep, who was pretty hot herself. But Leonard had been drooling for her, so Bernard would leave that particular piece to his coworker and friend.

"You rang," Meosha said as she walked into his office a few minutes later. Her hair was pulled up into some type of twist at the top, then left to hang long and straight down her back. She was a milk-chocolate complexion with the sexiest eyes he'd seen in a long time. Her lips were plump and could wrap around his cock like a thick blanket.

She closed the door and Bernard heard the telltale click of the lock falling into place. How many times had he fucked her in his office? On the couch? On the desk? In his private bathroom? Too many to count.

"I wanted to talk to you about us," he began after clearing his throat. Meosha wore a short black skirt that clung tightly to her ass and hips. Her blouse was yellow and not really office attire. It was sleeveless with a tie that came around her neck and led to her bare back. Her breasts were unbound, bouncing like crazy as she walked to his desk. Bernard felt his dick harden even though his intention was to break up with her, not fuck her.

"What about us?" she asked, sitting in the chair across from his desk and crossing her legs so that her tiny skirt rode up the remaining inches, giving him a free and clear view of her upper thigh and a good portion of her left butt cheek.

"It's time to move on, Meosha. We've both had fun but

I think we can safely say it's over." He'd said it, yet his gaze couldn't help but fall to all that exposed skin once more.

Meosha laughed. "Are you serious, Bernard? I mean, how can you sit there and say that with a straight face and a hard dick?"

"You don't know that I'm hard," he retorted, then shifted slightly, hoping to adjust the almost painful erection.

"Come on now, Bernard, we've been having fun for about three months now," she said as she uncrossed her legs, got up from her seat, and came around the side of his desk. "Don't you think I know when you're hot for me?"

She sat on the edge of his desk, lifting her foot to touch one pointy-toe shoe to the stiff length of his cock.

He caught her at the ankle. "It doesn't matter. It's over."

"You sure about that?" With his hand on her ankle she maneuvered herself so that she was still sitting on the desk but was now spread-eagle in front of him.

His gaze dropped to what was so blatantly being offered and Bernard swallowed hard. She wasn't wearing panties, but then he'd known she wouldn't be. She never came to his office wearing them; it was an unspoken rule they'd had since the beginning.

Looking up at her, he let his hand slide from her ankle, up her calf to her thigh. "This doesn't change a thing," he started saying just as his fingers touched her clean-shaved crotch.

She sucked in a breath and scooted closer to the edge of the desk, falling back on her elbows. "It means I'm going to have you inside me again."

Bernard stood, as his fingers steadily parted her already moist folds. His other hand had gone to his belt buckle as he quickly released his throbbing erection.

"It means this is finished." The fact that he was whipping out his cock and reaching for one of the condoms he kept in his bottom drawer did not deter him from his goal.

She fingered herself as he covered his cock with the latex. "Hurry, I'm burning up."

And that she was, Bernard thought as he looked down at her. Meosha Cannon was one hot piece of ass. But he'd tapped it long enough. This would be their farewell. She'd served her purpose with him and now he would move on.

Bernard was crazy if he thought she was letting him go that easily. They weren't finished until she said they were finished, Meosha thought as she tilted her hips and welcomed his long cock inside her sweet walls once more.

He had no idea who he was dealing with. Yeah, they'd both entered this office affair knowing it was temporary, but now Meosha had higher ideas. She moaned as his pace quickened, putting two fingers into her mouth and then reaching around and touching them to his balls, fingering the tight bags between them. He groaned and she pumped with him.

In another few minutes he'd thrown his head back and emptied his release into that condom. Meosha pulled herself up off the desk, ripped the latex from his still hard erection, and went down to her knees. Bernard never finished completely inside her. He always needed her to take him into her mouth to really get him off. Today was no exception, she thought, as she took him deeper toward her throat than she had her pussy. He held onto her head and pumped her mouth fiercely.

Cutting her gaze up at him, she saw his face distorted with pleasure, his mouth partially open, his tie swinging back and forth with their movements. His stuck-up wife never did this for him, he'd told her so. The way Meosha saw it, Bernard needed her just as much as she needed him.

"Swallow it all, every last drop," he told her when he'd looked down at her. His hands gripped her face, now tilting her head so he could watch his dick going in and out of her mouth.

Meosha held on to the base of his cock as it pulsed, taking the spurts of cum and swallowing them just as he'd instructed.

"It's over," he repeated again as he pulled his wet cock from her mouth.

Meosha licked her lips and stood. "No. It's not."

She'd pulled her skirt down and left his office, not looking back at him and not giving him a chance to argue with her.

"You're a home wrecker."

An hour later, Meosha paused, turned around and stared at her best friend, Kalita, the minute she walked into the condo they shared. "I am not."

"You are sleeping with a man you know is married."

"Correction," Meosha said, putting a hand on her hip. "He's also sleeping with me and for the record he knows he's married too."

"Two wrongs don't make a right."

"And being right doesn't pay the bills," Meosha quipped, then turned away again. Kalita could be a judgmental bitch when she wanted to. Meosha knew what she was doing, she knew the kind of life she eventually wanted to lead and knew that Bernard Williamson could help her get there. The fact that he was married was only a small issue. Actually, in her mind it wasn't an issue at all.

Kalita continued to polish her toenails, not missing a beat when chastising her longtime friend. "So now you're a ho?"

"I thought I left my mother back in Chicago."

"You must have left your brain there too."

There weren't many people in the world that could talk to Meosha like that without her smacking the taste out of their mouth. But she and Kalita had been through the type of mess that would make best-selling books. To say they were tight was an understatement. They'd known each other since elementary school, sharing everything from secrets to pantyhose.

"Look, I don't say anything about that deadbeat dad you're fucking," Meosha finally returned as she retrieved a soda from the refrigerator and sat on a stool.

They subleased a condo in Fells Point that cost them a small fortune to stay in and obtain. But it was the lifestyle they were both determined to live. Kalita worked as a publicist for a major public relations firm. That had actually been how the two Chicago natives came to be in Baltimore. Right out of college Kalita had been offered an internship with Lifestyles, Inc. Two years after that they'd offered to move her to their home office where she could work on some of their high-profile clients.

Meosha had been using her business degree as an office manager in a medium-sized accounting firm. She liked the control of running an office, but instinctively craved more money and power. As the youngest of five children, Meosha was constantly being told what to do and how to do it. One thing she swore she'd always have in her adult life was control.

"At least he's not married," Kalita retorted with a roll of her eyes.

Kalita was five feet four with a butterscotch complexion. Her body was fit, a perfect size eight, as she worked out religiously. Her hair and nails were always done and she carried herself in a cool, understated manner. How she managed to pick up every gutter-talking lowlife man that walked the earth, Meosha had never understood. Luckily, she was smart enough not to get pregnant by any of them. The girl was just too damned softhearted for her own good.

On the other hand, Meosha had adopted an "all about me" mentality when her parents had mysteriously come up with the money to send her two older brothers and sisters to college and then become flat broke when it was Meosha's turn. All her life she'd received her sisters' hand-me-downs and in school she'd been constantly compared to her brothers because she wasn't as smart as they were.

She'd put herself through college by working as a waitress in a swanky uptown restaurant. Well, she should probably concede that a few key patrons to that restaurant and their generous tips had put her through college. That's when Meosha learned her greatest lesson to date, how to get ahead.

"I know what I'm doing, Kalita," she said, finally too tired from staying late at the office to continue arguing.

"That's what you think, Mee. But you can't keep playing with fire and never expect to get burned," Kalita said seriously.

She stood from where she'd been sitting on the couch and headed for her bedroom. Pausing, she looked over her shoulder for one final parting remark. "Just be careful."

"I'm always careful," Meosha stated matter-of-factly.

Chapter 3

"We're just fine like this, Casey. I don't see why you keep harping on that marriage thing," he said with a huff before plopping down onto the bed.

Simon Davis was not getting married. Not today and not any day in the near future. He was working on his modeling career, focused on his clothes and keeping his body in tip-top shape. Casey was his girl and he loved her to death, but he wasn't walking down the aisle, not even for her.

"What we're doing now is just like being married," Casey countered.

"Exactly. So why mess up a good thing?" He gave her that teasing smile that she'd come to love.

But Casey had learned in the last two years of their five-year-relationship that Simon's smile wasn't going to be enough for her. She wanted marriage and children. She did not want to be Simon's live-in girlfriend for the rest of her life. "I'm not doing this forever," she said finally. He'd turned his attention back to the television.

Casey had worked late tonight trying to make sure they

had everything in place for the trip to Antigua at the end of the week. All the while she'd been thinking of how she would give Simon this ultimatum she had no choice but to give.

"I like how things are right now, Casey. Besides, you've got your job. Things are happening for you at the company and I'm proud of you." He reached out, wrapped his arm around her shoulder, and pulled her closer to him on the bed.

Casey looked around the bedroom they'd shared for five years. It was cluttered with things they'd collected, memories they'd made. The walls needed a fresh coat of paint but the furniture was still great, heavy, sturdy, dependable oak. The sheets were always a mess on the bed because Simon never made it up and Casey left the house before him. Even coming home late they were still rumpled with him lying on them watching television. That was Simon's favorite hobby, next to lifting weights and studying his physique.

She loved this man with every fiber of her being. Still, she inhaled and began to speak. "I'm going out of town for business this Friday."

"Oh yeah?" Simon's voice perked up as he figured they were finally off the marriage subject.

Casey hated to burst his bubble. "Yeah, we're shooting that Panzene commercial I was telling you about in the Virgin Islands."

"Damn, the Virgin Islands. Can you take guests along?"

"No," Casey answered quickly. She really didn't know if she could or not, but she didn't want Simon to go. That probably seemed cruel but she'd decided last week that if they got this account she would use this time wisely. "It's strictly business and we're on a tight schedule to get all the shots and get back to the office to kick off this campaign."

"That's cool, boo. I have a photo shoot lined up for Saturday. With this new portfolio I'm building my agent should be able to get me some better gigs."

Simon made pretty decent money with his modeling, he paid his share of the bills and treated her as often as he could, so she wasn't complaining in that area of their relationship.

"So while I'm away I need you to think about some things."

Simon exhaled. "Casey, this room does not need to be painted. I just painted it last year."

"I'm not talking about the paint."

"You're not. Then what?"

"I want you to consider marrying me or losing me." When he opened his mouth to speak, Casey put a finger to his lips. She leaned forward and kissed the mouth she was so familiar with. Simon was a very attractive man with his thick black cornrows and dark eyes. He looked almost like Shemar Moore, but better, in her eyes. And he was a good man. In the time they'd been together Casey hadn't had the drama of cheating or exes calling and stalking him. He was her man and she'd been secure in that fact. It just wasn't enough.

"You've known since the beginning the kind of life I want to lead. We've shared all our hopes and dreams with each other. I never said I wanted to shack up with you forever. Moving in together was supposed to bring us closer to marriage." Casey sighed. She should have listened to her churchgoing mother, who had warned that giving him the milk for free would surely set him against buying the cow.

"I want to get married and I'm tired of negotiating."

"Casey . . ." he began.

"Just think about it, Simon. Really think about it. Are your fears or hang-ups about marriage bigger and more important than keeping me in your life? Because if they are, then be prepared to watch me walk out that door. I won't stay with you if we aren't getting married. I just won't."

With that, she'd slipped off the bed and headed to the shower. It had taken a lot for her to put that choice out there because Casey knew that whatever the outcome, she would have to stand by it. If he chose to walk, then she would be alone. She had no idea where she would live or even if she could afford to live on her own, but she'd meant what she said. She was prepared to give up the five years they'd spent together if she couldn't have the future she wanted. It was as simple as that.

Leonard parked his Mercedes Roadster behind Lisette's white Cadillac Escalade in the driveway beside the Williamsons' house.

He hardly ever came here when Bernard wasn't at home. But tonight he couldn't resist. Bernard was in his office with the door locked. Leonard knew because he'd tried it on his way out when he was going to ask Bernard if he wanted to go get a drink. If Bernard's office door was locked that meant he was screwing somebody at work. That's how Bernard got down. And for a few years Leonard had idolized him for the chances he took with their coworkers.

However, in the last year, that idolization had turned into something else, pity and just recently a low, simmering rage. Leonard wasn't normally one to begrudge a man from getting as much ass as he possibly could, because he certainly did. It was the fact that Bernard had been cheating on Lisette for so long that pissed him off. If he didn't want her he should just leave her. That's what Leonard did when he was finished with a woman. So he didn't really care who Bernard was knocking off tonight, Leonard just wanted him to finally divorce Lisette so he could be the man she truly deserved. For Lisette Williamson, Leonard would turn in his playa card forever.

As he walked to the door his heart beat faster. He was going to see her again. Leonard made it a point to see Lisette Williamson at least two times a week. He knew her schedule as well as he knew his own, so appearing at the gym when she was there or just happening to show up at or in the vicinity of the women's center where she volunteered on Thursdays had become a part of his ritual. For a year the glances and friendly conversations he managed to share with her had held him content. Until recently, when every woman Leonard plunged his cock into had the same face: Lisette's.

It was crazy, he knew. She was another man's wife. His friend's wife. By all technicalities she was off-limits. His mind knew that, but his heart had ideas of its own.

He knocked and waited.

She answered and all sane thought fled from his mind.

"Hi," he said when the silence seemed to linger too long.

"Hey, Leonard. Come on in," she said then stepped aside.

"Thanks, Lisette. I was on my way home," he began, after she'd closed the door and they stood in the foyer of Bernard's single family home. "But I wanted to stop by to see if you needed anything. I know Bernard's working late tonight; he was still at the office when I left." That wasn't exactly snitching on his friend so Leonard didn't feel one ounce of guilt.

"Oh," Lisette's small mouth pursed, then she looked away. "He didn't tell me he'd be late."

No. He wouldn't have, Leonard thought, that rage bubbling just a little bit more. "Well, if you need anything you know all you have to do is ask."

Lisette turned back to him and smiled. Her long, straight auburn hair was pulled back into a ponytail, her golden-toned skin free of makeup and her slim frame sexier than ever in slacks and a blouse.

"No. That's okay. I'm fine, Leonard. But thanks for stopping by to check on me."

"You know I'd do anything for you and Madison." *Anything* was an understatement, Leonard thought. How many nights did he spend imagining that this family was his?

"You're a good friend," she said, stepping toward him and placing a hand on his arm. "I'll tell Bernard you stopped by."

Leonard nodded but wanted desperately to pull her into his arms, kiss her and make her forget there ever was a Bernard Williamson in her life. But he refrained. "Nah, it's no problem. Bernard would do the same for me."

"If you ever get around to finding a woman to settle down with," Lisette said before opening the door for him.

"I think that woman's hiding from me," he said.

"No, she's not. You're just not looking in the right places."

Leonard stopped in the doorway and turned to stare at her. He was looking in exactly the right place. "Good night, Lisette. And remember, if you need anything while Bernard's at work, don't hesitate to call me."

She nodded, her lips spreading into a smile and Leonard felt a tightening in his chest, the swell of love for this woman growing.

"I will. Don't worry about me and Madison. We'll be fine."

"Good night, Lisette."

"Good night," she said and watched him until he got in his car and beeped his horn as he backed out of her driveway.

He couldn't help but worry about her and her daughter, just as he knew he wouldn't be able to help but dream about her tonight.

Lisette Williamson. Another man's wife. And the woman of his dreams.

It was late, much later than Bernard normally came home from work. He'd stayed in his office long after Meosha had left, thinking about what he'd gotten himself into with her. There was no question that he had to do something about her, but what?

Now he was home, his house quiet since it was well after midnight. Taking the winding staircase, his footsteps grew hushed when he stepped onto the carpeted floor in the hallway and moved toward his daughter's room. The door was ajar, the glow of a pink Cinderella castle night-light emanating from one corner.

Stepping through the door, he stopped and watched her. Sound asleep, her tiny body seemed to be drowning in the plush pink comforter and numerous pillows. Peeking from beneath the comforter was the red yarn hair of her favorite doll. Ms. Kim, she called her.

Bernard's chest warmed. This was what he lived for, what he worked for, all he truly cared about. His little girl. Taking a step toward the bed, he stopped and bent down, placing a soft kiss on her forehead. She stirred, opening one eye to peek up at him.

"Hi Daddy," she said in her sleep-groggy child's voice.

Bernard smiled. "Hi, baby. Go back to sleep."

"You go to sleep too, Daddy," she said as her eyes closed again.

With another kiss Bernard moved from the bed and left Madison's room. Walking slowly down the hall to where he slept with Lisette he felt only mild guilt over the fact that he'd just fucked another woman. It was what he had to do. He'd gotten himself into this situation with Lisette, this marriage of convenience that she wanted to build into something else while he wanted to run as fast as he could in the opposite direction. But for him, because of the little girl asleep in her bed, there was no way out of this situation.

Divorcing Lisette was not an option. Not for his daughter, who deserved both her parents together in her life and not for his career.

So, for now, the decision was to keep on going the way he had been. And as he opened the door and stepped into his room he resigned himself to his fate.

He thought she was asleep, no doubt, but Lisette Williamson watched knowingly as her husband, the man who had promised to love, honor, and protect her walked into their bedroom without saying a word to her. He took off his tie, moved to the walk-in closet they shared and hung it on the tie rack next to the almost two hundred others he had. Then he went to his dresser, grabbed some underclothes and headed for the shower.

All she could do was shake her head. This was her life. It had been for the last seven years. She and Bernard were like strangers. Which, in the beginning, was a puzzle to her. When her sorority sisters had dared her to pick a random dorm room, knock on the door and flash the guy who answered, she'd thought nothing of it. All she had to do was open her coat quickly, display her naked body for all of two seconds, then turn and leave. Just a simple game in the life of college students.

But Bernard had answered. His smoldering gaze had held her transfixed. So when she opened her coat it had been more like a movie in slow motion than a quick flash. He'd taken one look at her and pulled her inside. The rest of the night was full of soft moans and deep thrusts.

He was the first stranger she'd slept with but the next morning she hadn't felt a bit ashamed. She and Bernard spent a lot of time together after that until Lisette felt herself slowly falling in love with him. When she found out she was pregnant she was ecstatic and then she was afraid. Bernard was adamant about wanting a career, to stabilize himself before making any type of relationship commitments. A baby was definitely a commitment.

But he'd married her anyway and Lisette thought that meant they were going to try and make this work. How wrong she'd been. The scorching hot sex they'd shared in college cooled significantly after Madison's birth. For a while it had cooled so much she'd been convinced he was sleeping with someone else. Then when Madison turned a year old Bernard had taken her for a week in Hawaii. She'd thought their relationship had been jump-started, but then they'd returned home and he went back to working late and turning to her less frequently.

In the past five years sex with Bernard was sporadic at best and always when she initiated it. It was as if without her request he wasn't interested, like he was doing her a favor by simply being here. Lisette had spent the last few years wondering what she could do to save her marriage, praying that there was some way she could reawaken the life she and Bernard had shared in the beginning.

Then she found it.

A black thong tucked into the inside pocket of one of

his suit jackets. For endless moments she'd sat paralyzed on the edge of their bed, the suit jacket in one hand and the thong in the other.

It was confirmation. Validation. Irrefutable proof that her marriage to Bernard was in trouble.

Sure, she'd considered the possibility of him cheating on her in all the years they'd been together but she'd always held firm to the fact that without proof she would not throw her marriage away. Now, she had that proof. What did she plan to do with it?

Two weeks ago she'd been having lunch with Ananda Cannady. Ananda was married to Congressman Benjamin Cannady of the Fifth District. The one who just last month had been in the news for being caught in a hotel just off the Beltway with a twenty-year-old stripper. Lisette remembered feeling bad for her friend when she'd watched the newscast, but sitting across the table from Ananda that day she would have never guessed the drama that had just gone on in the woman's life.

"Girl, I'm not mad or hurt. Ben got just what his trifling ass deserved . . . caught up," Ananda had said then threw her head back, laughing.

"But how can you be so calm? You've been married to him for fifteen years." Ananda's actions were too strange to accept.

"I can be calm because I knew he'd been running around with that slut six months prior to his ass being caught. Actually, I planned the ultimate exposure of his little tryst."

"What?" What Ananda said wasn't making a lot of sense. What woman set her husband up to get caught on national television with his pants down?

A betrayed woman. A hurt and determined woman.

Ananda had explained how she'd hired this woman from a company called Breakdown, to do exactly that to her husband. This woman apparently followed Ben around, got all the goods on him then somehow worked it so that the news crews and anybody else who cared to see—including Ananda, who was disguised in a car on the other side of the hotel parking lot—was there when she called the police and had the door to the hotel kicked in. The fact that the stripper Ben had been sleeping with was also connected to a money-laundering ring at the spot where she worked was only icing on the cake.

It was the craziest thing Lisette had ever heard. Until Ananda continued. Ben had been given the opportunity to stop the relationship and give Ananda an amicable settlement for her pain and suffering. Instead, he'd brushed off the warnings and told Ananda she was free to go whenever she wanted, but that all she would get from him would be decided in court. Just like any other lying-ass politician, Ananda knew that the bulk of Ben's assets were hidden and that she'd never get her share. So her only recourse was to break him down before she divorced his ass then kick him in the financial balls.

"You know Bernard is cheating. You know what he's worth. And you know what will happen if he's exposed," Ananda had said pointedly before stuffing a cream-colored business card into Lisette's hand. "Get his ass before he continues to get you."

Two days later Lisette was still struggling with how she was going to deal with her philandering husband. There was no question about Bernard's infidelities nor how much pain they'd caused her. Her biggest issue was whether or not she was willing to give up everything she had, the home she'd created and her daughter and the lifestyle they'd become accustomed to. Not to mention the scandal a divorce would undoubtedly be. Was she really willing to let another woman take the man she'd planned her future with?

The ringing phone snapped her out of her deep thoughts and she sighed as she reached to pick it up. It was the building manager of an apartment complex in downtown Baltimore. An apartment complex where Bernard was renting an apartment.

Lisette completed the call while she raged from within, then stood to go into her bedroom. Finding her purse, she pulled out the cream-colored business card with the words BREAKDOWN, INC. in lavish script. Without another thought she picked up the phone and made the call.

That was a week ago, Lisette thought as she watched Bernard return from his shower. His golden skin still glistened with beads of moisture, tempting her to touch him. Yet Lisette only had to close her eyes to picture some other woman touching him. Kissing his rippled abs, or riding his thick cock. Bernard loved to be ridden into pleasure. And the fury raged within.

How dare he treat her like this, then walk around like it was no big deal! How dare he toss away all that she'd tried to build for him, for Madison, for their family!

He was a deceitful bastard and she vowed to break his cheating ass if it was the last thing she did.

Chapter 4

"If you're finished with her I can take her off your hands," Leonard said, taking a seat in the guest chair across from Bernard in his office at CCM.

Bernard leaned back in his chair, rubbing his hand over his smooth-shaven chin. It was early Tuesday morning and Bernard was contemplating the colossal mistake he'd made by fucking Meosha in his office again last night. "Nah, you don't want to bother with that. I should have known she'd be bad news."

For a moment Leonard only stared at him, then gave a stilted chuckle. "Good pussy, but bad business."

"It was never business," Bernard confessed. "She was a good assistant and now she's a passable copywriter, but she'll never get any further than that. She doesn't have the balls to run an ad campaign the way we do at CCM."

"I didn't think so. I mean, she seems smart and everything, but she doesn't have that edge. Now, that Casey, she's pretty good."

Bernard's eyes opened just a tad wider and he tried

like hell to put a check on the warning about to roll off his lips. Leonard was a good friend, Bernard shared things with him he wouldn't dare share with the other stuffed shirts in the office. But Casey, she was not to be shared. Not with anybody.

"She's catching on. I want to see how she works in Antigua."

Leonard nodded, brushing the lapel of his dark-colored suit as if there was something there. "Yeah, we've got a tough timeline. Censor wants us back here in a week."

"We can shoot a commercial in a week. That's not a problem."

"But we'll be working night and day. That won't give me time to find all that tropical ass I plan on tapping."

The men laughed with Bernard agreeing he'd definitely have to work some time into his schedule to begin his seduction in earnest of Casey McKnight. She wasn't going to know what hit her and by the time they were on the plane heading back to Baltimore, her live-in boyfriend would be looking for another home.

The fact that his pursuit of Casey could potentially break up her home didn't bother Bernard in the least. He was a man used to getting what he wanted. And he wanted her. There was no doubt about that. And, just as he'd admitted to himself a few seconds ago, he wasn't sharing.

"So what do you think?" Leonard was saying.

"What?" Bernard tried to shift gears, to pay attention to the conversation with Leonard instead of daydreaming about his time away with Casey. "What do I think about what?"

"Man, you're not even paying attention to me."

"Sorry, had something else on my mind. Go ahead, tell me what's on your mind."

"I was thinking about that sexy honey from Panzene. She's going to be down at the beach. I'd love to get a taste of that."

Bernard nodded. She had been fine, and seemed vaguely familiar. "You get any vibes from her when we went to lunch?"

"It's funny, but I think I did."

"So why's that funny?"

"A couple times I thought she was eyeing the waitress just as much as she was eyeing me," Leonard chuckled.

"For real?"

"Yup." Leonard nodded. "But that's cool if she swings both ways. I'm not tryin' to marry her, just get my thing off a time or two."

Bernard gave him a knowing look. "Or three or four."

Leonard smiled broadly. "You know it."

Bernard did know it and had similar plans of his own. Two more days, that's all he had left, then he would be thousands of miles away from Lisette and just a wall away from Casey. He'd made sure his assistant booked all the rooms; in turn, he'd made sure that Casey's room was right next to his.

He wanted her close and he wanted her now. His fingers itched to touch her bare skin, his mouth watering at the sight of her luscious, naked body. He had it bad, he knew, but all this waiting and wanting was about to end. By this time next week he would have her. When he planned to let her come up for air he had no idea. The point was she would finally be his.

Casey frowned as if Simon could see her face through the phone. Ever since she'd given him the ultimatum last night, he had been trying to get her to see his side of the story. But she refused to back down.

"That's no excuse, Simon. If you love me—"

"Come on, Casey, we're not kids. Stop playing that tit-for-tat shit. You know I love you. I've been with you for five years now. While our friends were breaking up and starting new relationships you and I stayed together. There's something to that, something to this thing we have together."

"I'm not disagreeing with you but this 'thing' needs to progress. We've been in the same position for years. If we don't move forward, then what? We stay boyfriend and girlfriend forever?"

"Is that a crime? I mean, I'm not cheating on you and you're not cheating on me so what's wrong with what we have going?"

She exhaled and closed her eyes. "What's wrong is that it's not what I want anymore."

The line was quiet for a few minutes. "So you don't want me anymore. Is that what you're really trying to say, Casey? If so, just say it. We've been together too long to play games."

Casey was about to tell him he was talking crazy. Of course she wanted to be with him. Why bother with an ultimatum if she didn't want to stay with him? But before she could speak there was a quick knock on the door to her small office, then Bernard Williamson, her immediate supervisor, poked his head inside.

"I need to speak with you. Is this a bad time?" he said in that velvet-smooth voice of his.

Casey was shaking her head and waving him into her office at the same time as telling Simon, "I have to go. We can talk about this later."

"I'll be here," Simon said, then disconnected, leaving Casey feeling momentarily bereft.

"Sorry to interrupt," Bernard said, closing the door behind him. "You could have finished your call and come to my office afterward."

Casey was placing the phone back on its base. "No. It was nothing I can't handle later. So what did you need me for?"

A loaded question if ever he'd heard one. Bernard slipped his hands into his pockets and stood on the other side of her desk. She looked perfect today. Her brown hair was falling in deep waves down to her shoulders, her simmering brown eyes looked up at him and her pert lips spread into a smile. The simple, understated white blouse she wore had three buttons nestled tightly between her breasts. His gaze fell there, then reluctantly lifted back to her face.

"Just wanted to know if you were all set for the trip? Is the copy ready? The crew scheduled?"

She was nodding as he spoke. "Yes. I've checked and rechecked everything to make sure. I know we'll be on a tight schedule."

"Not too tight, I hope," Bernard said. "I was hoping for some downtime."

Casey sat back in her chair, trying not to be overwhelmed by how sexy Bernard was. That was easier said than done. Bernard Williamson was just about as fine as they came. Rich and down-to-earth to boot. While his financial status wasn't a big thing in her mind, the fact that he acted like your average Joe always made Casey feel comfortable around him—even on those days when he looked at her as if he wanted something more.

Similar to the way he was looking at her now.

"Maybe you should stay another week, make a vacation out of it," she suggested. "You've worked really hard on this campaign. After the commercial is finished I can come back and assist Leonard with the edits."

His eyes seemed to darken as she spoke, his stance changing so that his legs were slightly spread, his hands still in his pockets pushing his jacket back for an unfettered view of his broad chest.

"That would be perfect. If . . ." He let that last word linger in the air.

Was it hot in here? Casey sat straight up in her chair, trying like hell to keep her eyes on his and not on his tightly muscled body. He was wearing the rust-colored suit today, with the peach shirt and rust silk tie. He looked like a million dollar's worth of sex appeal, poured succinctly into a six-foot-three-inch body topped off with deep brown eyes and a killer ass.

And he was married. A husband and a father.

"If what?" she heard herself asking while her body experienced one of those hot flashes brought on only by his presence. It was crazy, she knew. She was in love with Simon. She wanted to marry Simon. And Bernard had his wife and family. Still, he looked at her as if . . .

"You could use a few days of R and R as well. I've been nothing but proud of your work on this account." He took a step closer to her desk and Casey was forced to note the fluid way with which he moved.

"I'm fine. I can wait until the holidays to take some time off."

"What if I asked you to stay a few days extra in Antigua to . . . ah . . . work?"

The question itself could be construed as slightly innocent, but the way he looked at her, the way his tongue crept over those sexy-ass lips, she knew there was nothing innocent about it.

"I don't know what we would work on," she said and wanted to kick herself for sounding like a fool. She was a grown woman and she knew when a man was coming on to her. Acting like a naive child was just plain ridiculous.

"You're staring at me, Casey."

"I am? Sorry."

He shook his head. "No. Don't apologize. Do you like what you see?"

Her lips moved nervously as she tried to smile and play off the heat rising up her neck to claim her cheeks. "Bernard, you know you're a good-looking man. Your *wife* knows you're a good-looking man."

He winched slightly at her words. Bernard didn't know what Lisette knew, and right at this very moment he didn't care. It wasn't Lisette that he was trying to fuck.

"I'm asking if *you* like what you see?"

And lying is another one of those dumb-ass stunts that only a teenager would pull. "You're a very good-looking man, Bernard. How could I not like that about you?"

He smiled, nodded his head then stepped around the side of her desk. "And you're a beautiful woman."

"Thank you," she said, moving only slightly so that they weren't as close.

That was futile because he kept coming closer until her chair that was scooting along the mat on the floor had backed into the wall. Grabbing the sides of the chair, he leaned forward until they were eye to eye.

"We both like what we see. We've liked it for some time now. I'm putting you on notice that once we're in Antigua my wife and your boyfriend cease to exist."

"Bernard," she began to speak and he moved in a little closer. He could kiss her right now. He could put his lips on hers and stop the words of denial he knew were about to come. Instead, he shifted gears. He was close enough that she would expect him to kiss her.

He extended his tongue, traced the line of her lips then said, "You and me, Casey. That's all. For one week, just you and me."

Casey was already shaking her head negatively.

"Don't," he warned. "Not right now. Just don't." Then

he stood so that his erection was what she was glaring at instead of his face. Reaching a hand out, he grabbed himself, massaging the thick length as she watched him, wanted him.

"I've wanted you so long," he began. "Some days I can't even think straight knowing you're just down the hall." With his free hand he traced her lips. "I know you're feeling me too."

He was too damned smart for his own good. The immoral thoughts she'd had about this man were ever foremost in her mind each day she stepped off the elevator to come to work. But she loved Simon and Bernard was married.

"Bernard. I don't think.—"

"That's right," he said, pressing a finger to her lips while still massaging his dick. "Don't think. Neither one of us will think once we're in Antigua. I mean it, Casey, once we land, all bets are off."

Casey, no longer able to sit in that chair with his finger on her lips and his erection poised in her face, stood on shaky legs. "Whatever it is we're feeling can never go further. Neither one of us is in a position to take it any further."

Standing was a mistake as she figured out the moment his arms went around her waist. She was pulled flush against his hard body, that magnificent erection now poking into her stomach.

"Tell me you don't want this," he said, thrusting himself into her. "Tell me."

She closed her eyes, loving the feel of him, wanting nothing more than to spread her legs and let him in. But she knew better. This was lust and just like with Simon she wanted more than their live-in relationship, she needed more in her life than this basic feeling. Bernard wanted to fuck her and if she were really honest with herself, she wanted to fuck him. Beyond that there was nothing else, which meant it was a waste of her time.

"I'm not about to lie to you," she began. "I want it. But I'm smart enough not to take it. Like I said before, you're married and I'm.—"

"You're what? Are you getting married? Are you on lockdown? Because until you have a ring on your finger, baby, you're fair game."

Casey tried to wiggle out of his embrace. Instead, she reached around behind, pulling his left hand until they both could see it. "But you're not. See this ring, it means something."

"To somebody else, it does," he admitted.

"What are you saying? Are you and Mrs. Williamson getting a divorce?" She hadn't heard any rumors about it but then she tried to keep to herself at work.

Bernard didn't know how to answer the question. No, would have been the honest reply. But honesty was a sure way to keep Casey's legs firmly shut. She was harping on this marriage thing so much that he knew it was going to be much harder seducing her with Lisette in the way. So Bernard did what any other red-blooded man with an erection that he feared would drain all the life from him would.

"Yes. We're getting a divorce."

"Oh," was all she said.

Taking full advantage of her shock, Bernard put a finger to her chin and lifted her face. "So you see, like I said, once we're in Antigua it's fair game. We both are free to get what we want."

Casey opened her mouth to come up with another reason why what he was saying was utter nonsense, but this time he silenced her with his tongue, pressing persistently between her lips, dancing wildly inside her mouth.

And it was over.

If this sultry, mind-numbing kiss was any indication, not only would it be fair game, Antigua was going to be one hell of a trip.

Chapter 5

Nola was all packed, her suitcases by the door as she stood looking around her apartment. It was inevitable, she always forgot something when she went out of town. This morning she'd gotten up an hour earlier so she could take her time, collecting everything she thought she'd need. Still, she felt like there was still something she was forgetting.

It wasn't as if this was a personal trip, so it should have made packing easier, not! As she patted her jacket pocket to make sure she had her keys, then opened her Dooney & Bourke wristlet purse, ensuring she had both her business and personal cell phone. When she'd finally given up figuring whatever it was she was forgetting wasn't important enough to remember in the first place, she turned to open the door just as her house phone rang.

Sighing, she crossed the living room quickly, stopping at the cherrywood and glass end table where her cordless phone sat on its base and glanced at the caller ID. Dammit! It was her mother.

"Hey Mama, I'm on my way to the airport. I'll call you

when we land," she said quickly and hoped that would be enough to get her mother off the phone.

She should have known better.

"Well, you can spare a minute for your mother," Evelyn Evans said in a curt tone. "I mean, I only spent twelve hours in labor to bring you into this world."

And since then she'd spent thirty-one years reminding Nola of this fact. "I didn't say I had no time for you, Mama. I'm just on my way out."

"I just called to check up on you since you're too busy to call me."

"You know I'm trying to get my business off the ground."

"From what I've heard from Marsha that business of yours is going just fine."

Aunt Marsha was Cally's mother and Evelyn's sister. The Evans family was a close-knit one, with their roots in St. Michaels even though Cally, Serena, and Nola had moved to Baltimore once they'd graduated from college. No doubt if Aunt Marsha was giving her mother updates on the progress of Breakdown, the information was coming straight from Cally, which might not be such a good thing.

"I presume you're going away for work," Evelyn continued.

"Yes, ma'am. I'm leaving for Antigua this morning but I should be back some time next week." It was easier to just answer Evelyn's question, Nola had found. No sense in putting her off for too long; her mother was very persistent. A trait Nola had inherited from her.

"Antigua. Well, that sounds nice. Why don't you take a few days after your work to get some rest and enjoy yourself."

"That's not possible. I have to work this case."

"Breaking up another relationship, huh. You call that work?"

Here it was, the real reason Evelyn had called. "That's not what I do."

"That's the way I see it."

"And you're entitled to your opinion," Nola quipped, then sighed. "Look, it's obvious you don't understand my work, or my need to do this, so why even bother discussing it."

"Because I'm worried about you, that's why. And I just don't see why you want to waste that law degree by seeking vengeance for every wronged woman of the world."

"Not the world, Mama," Nola said with optimism. "Just Maryland."

"Still too sassy for your own good. All I'm saying is that you could be doing so much more with yourself. You could open your own law firm, try cases and settle down."

"Mmm-hmm, and find a man and get married and have children. Is that what you really want to say?"

Evelyn sighed wearily. "No. I'll say what I've been telling you all your life. I want you to be happy, to find some contentment, some peace in your life. You've been angry for so long, Nola. Don't you think it's time to put that anger to rest, to move on and find something for yourself?"

Now came the headache that usually followed conversations with her mother. With one hand Nola rubbed the center of her forehead, pushing away the short-clipped bangs. "I am content with what I'm doing, Mama. You just don't understand that my idea of contentment isn't the same as yours."

"You're content to meddle in other people's relationships instead of building your own. No, that doesn't sit right with me and I'm not ashamed to say it. I'm also not ashamed to say that your father was a fool, a no-good, selfish ass who didn't know how to handle the love or the child I gave him. But that's his loss. I don't want my daughter throwing her life away because of it."

They'd been down this road so many times before. Frank Brentwood was, just like her mother had stated, no-good, selfish, and immature. He'd left her mother when Nola was only three years old, just vanished, never to be seen again. On more than one occasion Nola had thought of looking him up, finding him and giving him a piece of her mind. But what good would that have done? He was still gone. She'd still grown up without a father. Her mother had still nursed a broken heart for more than twenty-five years.

To hell with him and all the other self-centered, idiotic men out there like him.

"I'm not throwing my life away. I'm doing what I think needs to be done."

"You're wasting time and wasting your talent. Not every man is like your father."

"And not every woman is like you." The moment the words were out Nola was sorry. She loved her mother, ten times more so because Evelyn had raised her to be strong and aggressive even though she was not. Her mother was the last person in the world she wanted to hurt. And at the same time she was the last person in the world she wanted to imitate. Nola had no intention of giving her heart so completely to a man so that the loss of him would devastate her for years. She had no intention of being any man's victim.

"I'm sorry, Mama. That's not what I meant to say."

"Yes it is," Evelyn said with a watery chuckle. "You don't mince words, Nola. If you say something that's what you mean."

"Mama, I love and respect you, I always have. I'm just not like you."

"I know that," Evelyn answered. "And I'm glad for it. But don't shut yourself out so completely from finding someone. There's a man out there that will complement you. I know it. You just have to let go of some of this anger so you'll be able to see it too."

Tired of this conversation and well on her way to being late, Nola said, "I hear you, Mama. I really do. I just can't deal with this right now."

"Okay. You go on your trip, but when you finish with this case, think about what I've said. Think about it long and hard."

"Yes, ma'am."

"Now you travel safely and call me when you land."

"I will."

"I love you, baby."

"I love you too, Mama."

And because she did love her mother, as she drove to BWI Airport, Nola did think about what Evelyn had said. She thought about it so much her mind seamlessly shifted to Gee and the commitment he was pushing for. The commitment Nola had no intention of making.

They had first-class seats; Meosha expected nothing less. She'd seen Bernard and Leonard standing near the door just on the other side of the boarding line. For a moment she'd contemplated going over to him, then thought better of it.

Bernard thought it was time for their fling to end. Meosha had other ideas. She'd called him Tuesday night after their tryst in his office. He'd let the call go to his voice mail. The next morning at work she'd e-mailed him. He hadn't answered and she didn't receive a receipt that he'd even opened it. She'd worn her black dress yesterday, the one that was made of this slinky material that clung to her without the appearance of being tight. Bernard loved it when she wore this dress. Or at least he used to.

Now, Meosha was used to games; she played them as well as the next woman. But never before had she been on the receiving end of the diss moves. She didn't like it. And Bernard was soon going to find out how his latest moves weren't going to benefit either of them.

Meosha had figured out that she could get more from Bernard then the promotion and the averagely good dick. He was positioned to take over CCM in the next five years, but if his marriage continued he'd be positioned for so much more. Already Arnold Winston was talking of a play for city hall. It was no secret that with his connections over the few years he'd been not-so-subtly moving Bernard into the same social circles he roamed with the thoughts of slipping him into the city councilman seat.

And when that happened, Meosha wanted to be right beside him, or anywhere within the office with him. No, she didn't want to be married to Bernard, or any other man for that matter. She simply wanted to ride the success train with him.

So Bernard now had two choices: He could keep up with the program or he could watch his marriage and subsequently his future at either CCM or in city hall fall apart. She was not to be played with and he was about to find that out.

Her traveling attire consisted of hip-hugger jeans and a simple black tank top. In this regard, less was definitely more, she'd thought when she'd checked herself out in the mirror this morning. The jeans molded her curves into a tight little compact form, her tits and ass creating an eye-popping effect. Her four-inch heeled black sandals only added to the sex appeal.

This was the second time they'd called for persons to

board; first-class passengers had been called immediately upon the doors opening. Still, Bernard and Leonard stood to the side talking as if they had no intention of boarding this flight. Meosha knew that wasn't the plan. Panzene was a huge account. They'd paid Georgette Gillian, some supermodel from the latest African American beauties calendar and Shai Jennings, the latest Heisman Trophy winner, a bundle of money for this commercial. Both of them were definitely getting on this plane.

Tired of waiting for them, she picked up her Gucci duffel bag, slipped it onto her shoulder, and walked past them in the slowest, sultriest way she could. As she passed, their conversation stopped. She wouldn't look at either of them. Not Bernard, because she knew if she made eye contact with him she'd want to say something. And definitely not Leonard, because he was a goofball trying so hard to be like Bernard it was almost funny.

The silent treatment worked well and she heard an audible sigh of delight from one of them. *Yeah, look at my ass, you know you want it,* she thought and handed the attendant her ticket, then marched through the boarding tunnel.

Arriving in the first-class compartment, Meosha saw that there were only three seats left, each one on the aisle. She didn't mind that much but she was a little disappointed. Her hope was that there would be at least one more set of two seats together: for her and Bernard, of course. With a frown, she had to make a decision as she knew they were about to make the last boarding call and Leonard and Bernard would be on their way onboard.

She could sit with Jerome, the tech guy and junior account exec, who was also on their team. He was passably cute but didn't have jack going for him but a future in a dark room surrounded by computers. Those types of men freaked Meosha out, so no matter how much money they were capable of making she didn't mess with them. For some reason she envisioned them in those dark computer rooms jerking off or spying into other people's offices and homes, watching them get their thing off. Either way, she wasn't trying to go there, so she passed his empty seat without blinking an eye.

Then there was a seat next to Kingsley Mason, the Panzene chick. She looked polished and professional, sitting straight up in her reclining seat with a laptop already opened. Hell no, she was not trying to talk business all the way to the Virgin Islands.

So that left the seat next to Casey, which Meosha actually thought might be a good thing. Casey was what some would call a "nice girl." She dressed well, always covering her assets, but her clothes were of good quality and she had an eye for fashion. Meosha didn't mind giving a female her props when it was due. When it wasn't, she had no problem breaking their tacky asses down either.

However, Casey didn't have to worry about that coming from her. Casey was actually in a professional position that some days Meosha admired. Being an account executive put her second in charge of some of the company's big accounts and right next to Bernard. He was her immediate supervisor so the two of them spent lots of time in closed-door meetings and such. Yet Meosha didn't perceive Casey as a threat. The girl was so meek and so obviously committed to her boyfriend that it was sickening. Going into her office was like opening up someone's high school yearbook, all the pictures of them neatly posed together in different stages of their relationship was nauseating. Why one woman would spend that much time with one man that didn't have anything going for him except his tight-ass body and that killer smile, was beyond Meosha. Where did he work again? Oh yeah, he was trying to be a model. She almost laughed but then figured Jockey could always use a model with his physique. Still, that wasn't enough of a financial incentive for her.

Meosha stopped next to Casey and smiled when the woman looked up at her.

"Hey girl. I was wondering when you were going to make it onboard. I saw you standing out in the lobby," Casey said with her usual syrupy-sweet voice.

This child really did need to be schooled. This world was full of piranhas of the male persuasion and right now Meosha knew Casey was being sucked in by one. Maybe she'd take this time they'd have alone on the flight to talk some sense into her.

"Oh, I had to talk to Bernard about something before we boarded," Meosha said, wanting Casey to know right up front that even though she was a few steps below her on the office food chain, she was still on a first-name basis with the big guys.

"Yeah, he and Leonard were out there discussing something heavy. I just left them alone figuring if it had something to do with the account they would have told me."

See, *gullible*. No, they wouldn't tell her, they'd fix the problem then blame her in the meeting with Mr. Censor, then her ass would be fired. That's why Meosha made sure to always keep her cards stacked on upper management. You never knew when you might need it.

Taking her seat, Meosha immediately fastened her seat belt because she didn't mess around with planes and crashing and all that drama.

"Oh, hello, Bernard," Meosha heard Casey say and looked up to see the object of her obsession standing directly above her. From her vantage point she could simply reach out and touch the dick that had provided her with so many episodes of pleasure. But not here, not now.

"Mornin', Bernard," she said in a voice that almost matched Miss Goody Two-shoes sitting beside her.

"Good morning," he said in that deep voice that rubbed along her clit with the same fierce heat as if it were his tongue or his finger.

To Meosha's dismay, Bernard hadn't looked at her as he spoke. His dark gaze rested on Casey. Okay, this mutherfucka was really pushing her. Glancing down quickly to make sure her generous cleavage was on display, Meosha lifted a hand to Bernard's arm for a light, but alerting, touch.

His gaze then flew to her, as she'd known it would. Bernard had always been very adamant about their discretion. So her touching him in the intimate way she'd been sure to do, on the plane where any of their coworkers could see them, was sure to ruffle his feathers. But did she give a fuck? Hell to the no!

"Is everything okay? You and Leonard seemed like you were in deep discussion out there."

Like she gave a damn what he and Leonard were talking about. Bernard tried not to flinch and pull away. Her fingers were running lightly up and down his arm. But pulling away would look suspicious. If he just stood, smiled and acted as if nothing were amiss she would get the drift and remove her hand.

Who was he kidding?

Meosha Cannon was a woman on a mission. Wasn't that what Leonard had told him just a few minutes ago when she'd pranced her big tits and plump ass in front of them? He was going to have to deal with her once and for all. But not today, not this week. As he'd told Casey in her office yesterday, this week was all about them.

"Everything's fine. We're just anxious to get things

started." Purposely he ignored Meosha's breasts. He'd seen, licked, sucked, and slipped his dick between the heavy mounds countless times before. Now, he was no longer impressed. "Casey's concept for the commercial is great. We're all very excited about her working on this project."

"Thanks," Casey said, trying like hell not to blush. Ever since yesterday when he'd touched her, kissed her, Casey had been thinking about Bernard Williamson. Her boss.

He'd said they were attracted to each other. If the heat soaring through her body as his eyes focused on her was any indication, she'd say that was an understatement. It was awful and she'd tossed and turned all last night as Simon lay beside her. She hadn't really done anything with Bernard but she hadn't put him in his place and sent his ass packing either.

She'd simply stood there, like a schoolgirl with a crush. Loving the feel of his hands on her, the attention he was giving her. It was insane, she knew, and didn't co-incide with the plans she had for her life. Never would she have considered herself the type of woman who would sleep with her boss, or even entertain that idea. Yet when she'd finally drifted to sleep last night, that's exactly what she'd done.

Instead of tracing a line along her lips with his tongue, he'd plunged deep into her mouth, kissing her until her panties were drenched, her nipples burning with need. He'd touched her intimately then, his fingers drifting between her legs, parting her, seeking her, finding her hot and ready.

Casey blinked and shook the memory from her mind. It was crazy. Bernard was off-limits to her and the sooner she told him that, the better she would feel. At her hip she felt her cell phone vibrate. Lifting it out of its case, she looked down at the screen to see a text message from Simon:

Have a great trip. Love S

"Is everything okay?" Bernard was saying. She looked up at him. His brown eyes had grown just a tad darker, his lips no longer smiling but casting a slight frown.

"Ah, yeah. Everything's fine. You should probably take your seat, they're about to start the flight instructions," she said with a nod toward the flight attendant, who now stood at the front of the cabin.

"Yes, Bernard," Meosha said, removing the hand from his arm, tracing her finger along the line of her breasts, stopping as she said his name, at the valley between her luscious mounds. Bernard loved to lick her there, then when it was nice and wet he'd tap the head of his dick right along that spot and command her to squeeze her breasts around his length. The look of lust in his eyes as he turned his attention back to her was unmistakable and with a triumphant smile, she continued, "You should take your seat. Right over there." She pointed to the row of seats on the opposite side of the cabin. The one where Bernard would have no choice but to sit next to Jerome, the IT geek.

Taking his seat, Bernard thought he may have to re-think the way he was going to handle Meosha. Never before had she touched him in public. They'd both been clear on the rules of their involvement. But something in the way she looked at him just now said that she had changed the rules.

And he didn't like it.

Another thing he didn't like was her getting chummy with Casey. It was certainly foolish, he knew, but he just didn't want Meosha tainting Casey's enticing innocence with her worldly whorishness. Because at the end of the day, that's exactly what she was. Bernard was sure that he wasn't the first man in an executive position that Meosha had slept with to get ahead and was even more certain that he wouldn't be the last.

He had no respect for women like her. She wasn't marrying material, not even serious relationship material. She was only good for one thing. And he'd had enough of that. It was time to move on, he thought, chancing a glance over at Casey.

She and Meosha were conversing. Well, Meosha was talking and Casey was listening, with interest. Bernard's gut clenched. No, Meosha wouldn't possibly tell Casey about their affair. If she did he would personally strangle her. A harsh thought but one that only signified how deep his obsession with Casey had grown.

He'd dreamed of her last night. Dreamed of taking her right there on the desk in her office. When he'd awakened in the morning, with a hard dick and a desire that almost choked him, he conceded that fucking Casey on a desk was not the way he wanted to take her. He wanted their first time to be slow, an exploration and a completion that he'd craved even longer than he'd cared to admit.

Lisette lay asleep beside him as he'd let his feet hit the floor. Leaning forward, resting his elbows on his knees, Bernard had dragged his hands down his face. What was he doing? He didn't love Lisette. Never really had. But she'd gotten pregnant with his child and her father could do wonderful things for his career. They'd talked about him deciding whether to enter politics or move toward taking over CCM. Bernard was sure he wouldn't get either if he left Lisette.

She'd turned over, rubbed her hand up and down his

back and he'd wanted to tell her right then that it was over. But ambition overrode emotion; it always had in his book. So when she'd scooted closer, her hand moving around to cup the stiffness of his cock, he'd sucked in a breath and lay back down.

And as his wife climbed on top of him, inserting his dick into her already slick pussy, Bernard closed his eyes and continued to dream.

They were in their suite at the resort, in the huge king-sized bed with soft coverings. A slight island breeze blew through the open patio doors, tickling their naked skin. He gasped when she settled down, burying his cock deeper inside her. She moaned his name and he gripped her hips. She said she loved him and he let the words be translated from one voice to another.

She began to ride and in his mind he chanted, "Casey. Casey. Casey."

Chapter 6

"How'd it go?" Bernard asked Leonard when they were walking toward the baggage claim together after their long flight.

"How'd what go?"

Leonard looked a little perplexed and Bernard laughed. "With the Panzene rep. I saw you throwing your best lines at her during the flight. Is she interested or what?"

His friend could only shake his head. "Man, I don't know. I know I was saying all the right things, she just seemed to hear me and not hear me."

"How do you know you said all the right things?" Bernard asked as they rounded the corner where he could now see the many carousels distributing suitcases.

"Come on now, B. You know I have a plan of attack for all the ladies. I follow that plan strictly and I get results."

Bernard was looking upward at the flashing signs to see which carousel they needed when out of the corner of his eye he saw Casey walking alone. "Yeah, I know about your plan and those phony-ass lines you think work on women. Listen, I'll catch up with you later," he said and didn't wait for Leonard to refute the success of his personal playa handbook. Bernard had heard more than enough about the rules and regulations to be followed by a playa that Leonard lived by. It was funny and more than entertaining but right about now, he had something else on his mind.

Catching up to Casey, he reached a hand around and tapped her on her left shoulder while going to stand at her right. She turned both ways then grinned at him.

"Hey. I'm just trying to find my way around this maze," she said.

"I know. I think we're down here," he told her, pointing to the carousel at the end of the walkway.

"It figures we'd be all the way at the end."

Her dark hair brushed her shoulders as she spoke and Bernard couldn't help but want to touch her. In due time, he told himself, all in due time.

After retrieving their luggage he and Casey went through customs, displaying their passports and dealing with the mundane tasks of entering into another country. They'd landed in St. John's at V.C. Bird International, which was part of the U.S. Virgin Islands, but since September 11th all airports were tight on security.

They stepped out into the intense sunshine of the day and both of them looked around in awe.

"It's beautiful," Bernard said, watching out of the corner of his eye for Casey's response to her first glimpse of the island.

"Antigua is the largest of the English-speaking Leeward Islands. Its temperatures range from the mid-seventies to the mid-eighties," she said, reaching into her bag and pulling out her sunglasses, slipping them onto her face.

Bernard chuckled. "You sound like a tour guide."

"Sorry," she said almost shyly. "I did a lot of research on the island for the commercial. If we're going to market Panzene's new line correctly we needed to know what would be the best locale. This is the absolute best," she finished wistfully.

Three limousines pulled up to the curb and the drivers stepped out, each of them holding signs that said *CCM*. Grabbing Casey by the elbow, Bernard quickly looked around to see if anyone else from their party had made it through customs yet. When he didn't see anyone he moved Casey quickly to the first car.

"Shouldn't we pair up?" she was asking as the first driver instantly came up to them, taking their bags and carrying them to the trunk.

"Nah, there's enough room for the rest of them to take the other two cars. Besides, I want a few minutes alone with you."

She stopped at the door and looked up at him. He couldn't see her eyes through the dark lenses but knew that she was studying him in that serious way of hers. Damn, he couldn't wait to break down that intense barrier she kept erected. Once he had Casey naked and in his arms, she'd think of nothing and no one but him.

"Stop thinking so much, Casey. Just get in the car. What can possibly happen with us riding to the resort together?"

Not ten minutes later the limo was moving, winding its way through the tropical streets of St. John's, heading to the Horizons resort. Casey was a little nervous about staying at the resort with its hedonistic atmosphere, but what better way to promote Panzene's newest line of cosmetics, aptly titled Seductive. She'd never been to a resort designed solely for one's pleasure and really didn't know what to expect.

The island was gorgeous, from what she could see through the tinted windows. Palm trees leaned as if accommodating the tourists that traveled to see them, providing snatches of shade beneath the glowing sunshine. It seemed almost strange to be riding in the closed-in limo instead of walking along the paved streets that winded along the shore. But then, this trip was about business, not pleasure.

This account was important to her; making a good impression was important. She worked hard to make sure that everything was going smoothly on the Panzene account. The campaign had been designed to focus on the natural ingredients in Panzene's products. The fact that there were a number of other cosmetics companies using all-natural products as well only made Casey's job more demanding. She'd spent hours doing research, examining the market, analyzing the highs and lows, until she, along with the other members of the team, felt they'd created the perfect campaign to give Panzene the leading edge. This commercial was just the next step up from the print ads, radio, and Internet promotions they'd already completed. It would, for Casey and the team, be the icing on the cake if all went well.

Just as her mind had settled on business, Bernard's hand settled on her knee. She'd worn a short swing skirt with a camisole and fitted sweater that she left open. In no way was she dressing to entice. Apparently, Bernard wasn't hard to please.

Better she should put a stop to any ideas he might have, something she should have done yesterday. So putting her hand over his, she looked directly at him.

"Look, Bernard, about what happened in my office yesterday . . ."

"Don't you dare apologize," he said instantly.

"I'm not." She sighed. "But I am going to say that whatever we were feeling isn't right. You're married and I'm . . . I'm in a committed relationship."

"I'm getting a divorce and your boyfriend refuses to marry you. I'd say that makes both of us damn near available."

How did he know about her and Simon's issues? It didn't matter. Facts were still facts no matter how he tried to distort their meaning. "I don't know what your situation is or how you deal with it in your mind. What I do know is that I care deeply for Simon, so I'm not about to do anything that would betray him."

Keeping his hand on her knee, Bernard squeezed, then scooted closer to her and touched his other hand to her chin. "You didn't say you loved Simon," he whispered then leaned in to kiss her softly.

Dammit, she didn't. Her eyes fluttered closed as her stomach didn't somersaults at his touch. "Don't twist my words, Bernard. This isn't right."

"It feels right," he said, then touched his tongue to her bottom lip.

"It feels . . . um . . ." *Come on, Casey say it! Tell him this feels dirty. Tell him you're not some office slut that's perfectly willing to fuck the boss in the backseat of a limo. Tell him—*

"It feels too good to stop." He smiled. "You don't have to say it, Casey. I'm feeling just as riled up as you. There's nobody here but the two of us, nobody will ever know."

What the fuck? Casey really did feel like a teenager sneaking behind her parents' back to neck with the pastor's son. Damn, that was a memory she thought she'd buried. The shame of what they'd done in the choir stand had been too much for her to stand any longer. Could this possibly compare?

Bernard slipped the hand from her knee up her skirt and she sighed. Hell yeah, this was beyond anything she'd dared do at the age of sixteen in the choir stand at Fullerton Baptist Church.

"Let me in," he whispered.

Casey opened her mouth to speak and his tongue dipped quickly into her mouth. At the same time her legs parted of their own volition. His hand moved further until he touched the rim of her panties. Deftly pushing them aside, Bernard stroked the plump folds of her pussy and Casey whimpered.

This was so wrong, so wrong indeed. But it felt so good. Why was that always the case?

Dipping his fingers into her wet center, Bernard groaned. "I can't wait to get inside you. Can't wait to taste you. Feel you. I want you so badly, Casey. So damned badly."

"Bernard," she heard herself whispering his name and closed her eyes. Behind her lids she saw two people, two women who looked the same but felt vastly different.

On the plane she and Meosha had chitchatted like females tend to do. Until Meosha had gone into a full-blown kick-Simon-to-the-curb campaign. How everyone in the office knew about her personal issues was beyond Casey, but she had to admit, Meosha had some pretty valid points. Why should she be and do what Simon wanted? Didn't she deserve her own happiness? This was her life, she had a right to live it the way she wanted.

"Give me more," Bernard was whispering as he trailed hot kisses over her cheeks, her chin, down her neck.

Casey opened her legs and felt herself stretching as he inserted another finger into her. His hand began pumping her slowly, then with slightly quicker thrusts and Casey felt as if she were going to explode.

"Tell me you want me, Casey. Just say the words, please," Bernard was begging.

His deep voice resonated throughout the interior of the limo and Casey couldn't believe her ears. This was her boss she was letting finger-fuck her into an orgasm.

His mouth closed over her shirt-covered nipple and she gasped. This would be the one and only time. This was as far as they would go. Bernard was right, nobody would know what they'd done in this car. Nobody but him and her. Just like nobody had known about her and the pastor's son.

Once they arrived at the resort she'd go to her room, get herself together and then it would be back to business. This . . . oh God, his fingers felt fantastic . . . this was not going to get out of hand. She was not going to go any further with him.

She couldn't.

She wouldn't.

This was it.

His fingers paused inside of her, his thumb flattened against her clit and his eager mouth returned to hers. The kiss was designed to stifle her moan. The movement of his fingers was designed to destroy her. And there, in the back of the limousine, with her boss, Casey had what was to date the most powerful orgasm to ever ripple through her core.

She was so fucked!

The island of Antigua was okay, Meosha surmised, for as much as islands didn't excite her. Meosha had come to realize that there were only two things in this world that excited her: money and sex—and usually in that order.

Bernard had given her the slip, and it appeared, so had Casey. She wondered if they were together. On more than one occasion she'd caught Bernard looking across the aisle at Casey. Meosha knew all the office gossip, that's how she knew about Casey and her man. Never had she heard anything about Bernard and Casey. Besides, Bernard had told her before that sleeping with women he personally worked with was not a habit of his. She was the exception. That, unlike any other smooth words, had made Meosha feel good. Actually, that had been just about the kindest thing Bernard had ever said to her. He was not shy about stating his limitations early on in the affair.

That's exactly what this was, he'd told her repeatedly, an affair. There was no love, no dating, no getting to know each other better. They were fuck buddies and that was it. For Meosha these guidelines had worked perfectly. Until now.

She'd spent an insane amount of time getting checked into the Horizons, which was probably due to the fact that she'd been trying to find out Bernard's room number and its vicinity to her room. When finally the short, balding clerk had gotten the glimpse of her cleavage she'd been trying to show him for the past fifteen minutes, he'd smiled and told her what she wanted to know.

She was the one smiling as she walked away. Bernard's room was down the hall from hers. They were scheduled for a dinner meeting at seven, which gave her about two hours to freshen up. So she didn't waste another moment but moved quickly to the elevators. When she arrived on the fifth floor and had just turned the corner to go to her room she was stopped by a sight that did something strange to her stomach.

Bernard had Casey pressed against the door. Yes, Miss Goody Two-shoes, the same woman who had whined the entire plane ride about loving her boyfriend and wanting to get married and start a family. Meosha took a step back behind the wall, then peeked around to continue watching them.

Hell no! Hell to the fucking no! That conniving little tramp was not going to push up on her man! Okay, well maybe that was taking it a bit too far. Bernard was not her man, but he was her meal ticket and Meosha wasn't about to let him slip through her fingers that easily.

So this was why he was trying to break things off with her, he wanted a piece of the virginal executive. Well, Meosha had news for him. This was not how this game was going to play out, not if she had anything to say about it.

But just as Meosha was about to make her presence known, she felt a hand at her elbow and turned to stare right into dark brown eyes that were all too knowing, all too fierce, and just slightly familiar.

The headache that had begun with the conversation with her mother was now full-blown, making Nola irritable and tired. After listening to Leonard come on to her during the plane ride and then watching as the rest of the CCM staff on this trip went on and on about this commercial and this job, she'd had enough!

To make matters worse, Gee called.

"Hey, sweetness. Just checking to see if your flight was all right."

Nola had rolled her eyes, then caught herself because she knew he couldn't see her. Gee had been calling her at least once a day for the past two or three weeks and she was getting tired of it. They weren't boyfriend and girlfriend yet he was carrying her as if they were.

"Yeah, everything went fine. I'm at the hotel now, getting ready to go to my room and try to take a quick nap. They've got this meeting scheduled in a couple of hours that I've got to go to."

"You sound tired. Why don't you blow the meeting and just stay in your room?"

Nola frowned at the phone, knowing exactly what Gee was trying to do. He'd looked up the resort on the Internet. He knew that it was a hedonistic resort with two buildings, one being an au naturel.

"I'll be fine. Besides, it's my job."

"I can't believe you're doing this. Just because one man burned you doesn't mean you have to take it out on the entire male race."

This was another conversation that she and Gee had on a regular basis. He didn't understand her need to open and run Breakdown. But then he was a man, so why should he? "You have your career and I have mine," she said simply.

"Being an attorney is your career."

"Being an attorney *was* my career. But when that foul-ass Mark or Drew crossed the line, I kissed that dream good-bye. This is a new day and a new me. If you don't like it, Gee, you can always walk."

"Whoa. Hold on a minute. I never said I didn't like you, Nola. Just calm down. I'm just saying that I don't like you running all over the world following behind some punk-ass dude who's fucking around on his wife. Because the first dumb-ass that thinks he can turn his fuckups on you and try to cause you some harm is going to be staring down the barrel of my Glock. And you know I'm not aiming for no fool's balls!"

No, Gee wouldn't aim for the balls the way she had. If he raised his gun, he was going to shoot to kill, not maim.

"That's not necessary, I know how to protect myself. Besides, by the time they figure out who I am and my part in their demise, they need to be focusing on damage control."

"I just worry about you, Nola. Is that a crime?"

It was if this worrying tied in to some feelings he thought he had for her. Nola's head was hurting, and she definitely did not feel like having this conversation. Better to just get him off the phone. "No. It's not a crime. Look, Gee, I've really gotta run." And as if to aid in her comment, her other line beeped. "Somebody's on my other line. I'll call you tomorrow."

"If you don't, I will," he said seriously.

"Okay. Bye."

Nola pressed the button, swapped calls and felt her headache pounding with even more persistence.

"Hey, Nola. This is Lisette again."

Yes, again. Lisette Williamson had called her three times this week. One day, pissed off at her husband and ready to castrate him herself. The next day, a little concerned about what would happen when he was caught. Nola was afraid to find out what she wanted this time.

"Hi, Lisette," she said, trying to sound interested.

"Listen, I was thinking last night. Actually, Bernard and I had a really good time last night. I think things might be getting better."

Dammit! It was one of those having-doubt days.

"So maybe we don't need to go this route. Maybe once this commercial is shot and this account is closed things will get better."

"I know you don't really believe that, Lisette. He's been cheating on you for years, not just the time he's been working on this account."

There was silence on the line.

"But if there's any chance that we can save the marriage. . . ."

"Why would you want to save something that he doesn't give a shit about?" Nola caught herself getting loud. She had to remember that Lisette was still the client, no matter how ditzy a broad she was. "I'm just saying that in my experience men like Bernard don't ever stop their cheating ways. He may take a break, give you some attention for a while, but he'll ultimately seek that outside relationship again. That's just how he's made."

"Bernard's a good man."

Sure he was, to his wife and a dozen or so other women in the Baltimore metropolitan area. "Listen, Lisette, I'm here now and I think I have a lead on the woman he's sleeping with. So just sit tight, I'll call you tomorrow with an update."

Lisette paused, then took a deep breath. "Okay, but just call me before you do anything. I mean, find out who she is and then call me and we can talk about the next step."

To hell she would. In Nola's mind, the end always justified the means. "Sure thing, Lisette. It's your call," Nola said with a smile, then disconnected the line, turning her cell phone off.

She had just stepped off the elevator when she heard a sound. Looking down the hall, she almost smiled as she saw the subject of her investigation doing exactly what she'd just told his wife he would be doing, gripping some woman's ass and thrusting his tongue down her throat.

Typical bastard!

Then she noticed who the woman was and almost gasped. This was unexpected. Nola was sure Bernard was sleeping with Meosha Cannon. She'd actually heard the woman, Meosha, talking on the phone while they'd all been waiting for the plane to board about having Bernard all to herself once they got to the island. Nola was certain this was going to be an open-and-shut case.

Now, however, it seemed the fireworks were just beginning.

As if that weren't enough, Nola's satisfaction was kicked up a notch when she spotted Meosha peeping around the corner watching the scene with Bernard and Casey. So with quiet movements, Nola moved down the hall until she was standing at the break in the hallway that offered Meosha her shelter. She was just in time because she could see that Meosha was fuming and about to go at Bernard with both barrels loaded.

Instead, Nola grabbed her by the arm and pulled her further around the corner.

"What the hell are you doing? What do you want?" Meosha spat as she turned to see that Nola was the one pulling her back.

"I'm saving you from a monumental embarrassment and perhaps from losing your job."

"What? You don't know what you're talking about," Meosha said, looking at Nola with contempt.

The woman was pretty, Nola had noticed that the other day at the meeting. Her slightly slanted eyes gave her an exotic appeal. Her skin was a rich, dark complexion, her mouth sensuous. But that was neither here nor there.

"I know more than you think." Nola still touched her arm, feeling waves of something akin to attraction filtering through her body.

Meosha must have felt the same thing or she was too pissed to notice because she pulled out of Nola's grasp and stumbled back into the wall. Nola followed, stepping directly in front of her, standing so close the tips of their breasts touched.

"He was fucking you and now he's fucking her," she said simply and raised a brow, waiting for Meosha's response.

"How did you—?" she began to ask then squinted at Nola as if trying to figure something out. "Who are you? And don't tell me Kingsley Mason because I know I've seen you someplace before. Someplace other than the office."

The feeling of attraction was intense and Nola, try as she might to ignore it because this was a job and not a chance meeting, moved in closer. There was something about women who were into other women, or women who were at least open to experimenting with other women even if they didn't consider themselves lesbians.

A look, a spark in the eyes when a woman you were attracted to stood near. There, she'd seen it flash in Meosha's eyes as she rubbed her breasts against her. Oh yeah, she was definitely interested. This job was turning out to be one of Nola's favorites.

When Meosha didn't make a move to get away from her Nola said simply, "I'll tell you my secrets, if you tell me yours."

Meosha's body relaxed against the wall. She straightened her back, pressing her breasts out further, touching Nola's more soundly. "What if I don't have any secrets?"

Nola smiled. "Oh, you do. I can see them in your eyes."

"Really? What else can you see in my eyes?"

She was going to fuck her, Nola knew this as surely as she knew her name. Where they would go from there was anybody's guess.

Leaning closer until Meosha's ear was just a tongue lick away, Nola whispered, "Desire. Lust. Revenge."

Chapter 7

Kalita Sheraton was sick and tired of being sick and tired. Life should not be this difficult—correction: a healthy love life should not be this difficult.

Her best friend and roommate had been right, her boyfriend was a deadbeat dad. Well, since he was actually now her ex-boyfriend she could call it more accurately—he was a dead broke, deadbeat dad with delusions of grandeur.

How Clint Tripp thought he was just going to move in with her with his unemployed ass owing more than fifteen thousand dollars to each of his three baby mamas was beyond her realm of comprehension. Sure, he could lick pussy like no other man she'd ever met, but even that wasn't changing her mind.

To hell with him!

It was Friday night and Meosha had left this morning for her business trip to Antigua. Business trip, hell, Kalita knew exactly what Meosha had planned while she was on that tropical island. And she only prayed Bernard Williamson knew what he'd gotten himself into. Meosha was hell-bent on getting everything she wanted out of him before their affair was over—by any means necessary.

So Kalita was all alone sitting on the couch after having just popped in one of her favorite chick flicks, *The Best Man*. If she had to be in this house alone tonight she could at least spend it staring at that fine-ass Morris Chestnut.

About forty-five minutes into the movie when Kalita was nice and relaxed in her nightshirt, the brownie and ice cream she'd bought from Friday's finished and the empty bowl sitting on the coffee table, the doorbell rang. It was after eleven so she was skeptical about getting up to answer it, then it rang again and she climbed off the couch. Because they were two females living alone in the city, Kalita and Meosha had been steadfast about self-defense classes and protecting themselves at all times. So when her bare feet hit the blond wood floors she crept around the back of the couch, then reached down to slip the baseball bat from beneath. Moving to the door, she looked through the peephole but couldn't see anything but the back of a man's head. Taking a deep breath and raising the bat in one hand, Kalita flipped the latch lock then turned the knob to open the door.

The man on the other side turned to her with a smile that quickly died. She tightened her hands on the bat and was prepared to swing.

"Whoa!" he said, holding up both hands as if she were the cops. "Hey, Kalita. It's just me, Cam."

Kalita had to squint her eyes since the interior of the house was dark and the light from the hallway was too damned bright.

He'd cut off his dreads, looked a little darker than the last time she'd seen him but as he lifted those thick eyebrows of his and cocked that grin she'd always thought was too sexy, she felt her arms lowering. "Cam? What are you doing here at this time of night?"

The bat now rested at her side as she moved to let him in. After locking the door she put the bat back in its place and moved toward the couch.

"I just got back in town and I wanted to see Meosha," he said, removing his leather jacket and tossing it across the back of the recliner.

Cameron Hunt used to own a couple of barbershops on the west side of Baltimore, until he and Meosha broke up last year and he'd sold the shops and moved to New York where the rest of his family lived. As far as she knew, Meosha hadn't talked to him in all that time so his arrival at this hour was a little strange.

"She's out of town," Kalita said, sitting back in her spot on the couch.

"Really? When's she coming back?"

Cam hadn't taken a seat but instead stood about a foot away from her on the couch. From her vantage point she could see that he was still working out, his slim frame highlighted by the dips and curves of well-attained muscles. His jeans hung low on his hips, but not so much that his underwear was showing like the younger generation was apt to do. The black T-shirt with some weird design on the front hung loosely but she could still see his upper chest definition. With his low-cut hair and those deep, piercing eyes he watched her. Kalita wondered if she should feel uncomfortable then tossed the thought aside. This was Cam, he'd been in and out of this house on a daily basis for the eight months that he and Meosha had been an item. He was like a brother to her.

"She'll be back on Thursday. Her job went to Antigua to shoot a commercial for this big account they have."

"Oh," he said and still didn't move.

When a few moments of silence ticked by and Kalita

noted the scene change in the movie from when Lance, Morris Chestnut's character, almost jumped across the table to tackle Quincy, Terrence Howard's character, she looked up at Cam with impatience.

"What's going on, Cam? Why are you here, standing in my living room looking like a lost puppy?"

He let out a whoosh of breath then slipped his hands into his pockets. "You never did bite your tongue, did you, Kalita?"

"Beating around the bush is a waste of time. So tell me what's up so I can get back to watching my movie."

Cam moved then, crossing between the coffee table and television to sit beside her on the couch. He rubbed his palms up and down his thighs, then looked at her.

"I need a place to stay."

Lordamercy! She just couldn't keep kissing that man. She couldn't keep letting him touch her. She couldn't stop thinking about him.

Casey flung herself facedown on her bed the moment she'd returned to her room from the meeting. The storyboards were done, they'd gone over them with the producer and were ready to start shooting first thing tomorrow morning. Until that time she could be alone with her tumultuous and betraying thoughts of another man.

As if some spawn of the devil were in the room with her laughing its ugly head off, Casey's cell phone rang. She reached across the bed where she'd dropped her purse and retrieved it.

"Hello?" she mumbled, not really in the mood for talking right now.

"Hey, you. What's up? You didn't call to say you'd landed safely or anything."

Hearing Simon's voice only added to the headache building at her temple.

"Sorry. I got caught up in the scenery." Which wasn't exactly a lie. Antigua was gorgeous and the Horizon was definitely a four-star resort.

"Yeah, I can imagine. Maybe you and I can take a vacation down there," he suggested.

Casey cringed. There was no way she'd ever be able to come back to Antigua without thinking of Bernard. "Maybe," she said unenthusiastically.

"So what are you doing now?"

Simon wanted to chitchat. Casey wanted to take a hot shower, and attempt to wash some of the betrayal off her body. "I'm about to go to bed. I'll call you tomorrow."

"Hey, wait a minute. That's all you have to say to me? I'm calling to check on you, to tell you that I miss you and you rush me off the phone."

Casey exhaled. "You're supposed to be thinking about what I said before I left," she snapped.

"Thinking about what?"

"You don't remember what I told you? The choice I gave you."

"Come on, Casey, be serious. We're adults, in an adult relationship, you really want me to sit here and consider your ultimatum?"

"Yes, I really do. I have plans for my life and they don't include shacking up with you forever." Did they include sleeping with a married man? Casey closed her eyes to that question. She knew the answer, or at least her brain knew the answer. Her body was drawing its own conclusions.

"I don't see why we have to keep going down this road."

"Because you keep putting us there."

"Me?" Simon's voice got a little louder. Casey's head

pounded a little harder. "You're the one bringing it up every two seconds. I just called to check on you, not to argue."

"There wouldn't be an argument if you would simply make your choice."

Silence invaded the line and Casey dragged a hand over her face. She didn't want to be having this conversation, not right now. But he'd called and she'd been irritable and, well, this was still an issue between them. An issue that needed to be resolved, sooner, rather than later, so she could move on.

To Bernard's bed?

That thought popped into her mind and seemed to grow roots. She sighed, thanking the Lord that mind reading wasn't one of Simon's strong points.

"Is it that simple for you, Casey?" he asked suddenly, his voice substantially softer than it had been moments before. "Can you really put five years of our life into one question, with a yes-or-no outcome?"

He made her sound like a coldhearted bitch, which Casey knew she was not. Didn't she deserve some happiness? Didn't she deserve the chance to follow her dreams? She loved Simon, so there was no question of whether or not she wanted to marry and spend the rest of her life with him. Suddenly, she realized he must not feel the same about her.

"It's as easy as it is for you to tell me you love me in one breath, then break my heart the next. I never lied to you, Simon. I never led you to believe that this type of relationship would be enough for me forever. If you knew you didn't want to ever be married, you should have told me that sooner. You shouldn't have let us go this far."

"I shouldn't have fallen in love with you, is that what you're saying?"

"Maybe we shouldn't have fallen in love with each other."

The ensuing silence became too much for Casey to bear. She was about to say good night to Simon when she heard a soft knock at her door.

What now? she thought dismally.

"Look, I've got to go."

"Casey," he began then went quiet once more. "Fine. Call me back when you get a moment."

"Okay," she said, knowing that the last thing she wanted was to call Simon back and finish this conversation. "We start shooting tomorrow so I don't know how much free time I'll have."

"Please try," he stated and a part of Casey's heart began to break.

"I will. Bye." Casey disconnected the call before Simon could say another word and before she could second-guess the stance she'd taken.

Slipping off the bed, she made her way to the door where there was yet another knock. She pulled it open and stared into Bernard's dark eyes. Somehow she'd known it would be him. He was repeatedly coming between her and Simon.

"This isn't happening tonight, Bernard," she said, too tired to wonder if it was the right thing or if she could possibly lose her job by turning him down. Casey didn't care. There was too much going on in her mind right now, too many issues to deal with. "I'm not sleeping with you."

For a moment he looked shocked, then the corners of his mouth lifted in a smile. "Relax, baby. As I told you before," he said, stepping inside her room and closing the door behind him, "you don't have to do anything you don't want to."

Casey backed away. "I don't want to have sex," she said.

Bernard nodded as he flipped the lock on the door in place. "Then we won't."

She let out a breath and turned away from him, dropping her cell phone on the table and moving toward the patio. Her room was really nice with its sage and tan color scheme. She had her own private patio complete with furniture and a view of the huge pool that occupied the center of the resort.

Her bed was positioned in the center of the room with the desk, sitting chair and minibar to the left, the walkway to the spacious bathroom to the right. With the patio door open the air was sea scented, the night breeze light and relaxing. Yet Casey was anything but tranquil.

She was worried about where things were going with Simon and even more so about this new attraction to her boss. Never before had she considered herself a woman who would be sleeping with the boss, and she didn't really like how it felt now.

Her career achievements so far were based on her own merit, her intelligence, and tenacity. Not because she had slept with anyone to get anywhere. With those thoughts, she turned back to face Bernard.

He'd removed the light sports coat he'd worn at dinner so that now all he wore were his cream linen pants and white shirt. His golden complexion seemed darker in the tropical setting, his broad shoulders and strong facial features more pronounced. She'd known he was handsome, that much was apparent back in Baltimore. But here, in the Caribbean, he was mouthwatering.

"Why did you hire me?" she asked suddenly.

"What?" He moved closer to her, stood at one end of the patio door while she held post at the other. Outside, even though it was close to midnight, guests splashed about naked in the pool. Horizons welcomed their guests au naturel, which Casey found mildly offensive but endured because she'd known about it ahead of time.

"My job, this account, were they all a ploy to get me into your bed?"

Bernard chuckled. "Let's see, I hired you almost two years ago and to date, you haven't been in my bed once. Believe me, I would have remembered if you were."

"I'm being serious."

"And so am I." Slipping his hands into his pockets, he stared at her acutely.

"Then what's going on? Between us, I mean? What is this?"

"This, I believe, Casey, is called attraction. You and I are undeniably attracted to each other."

"But it's wrong."

"Says who?"

Moving outside, Casey plopped down in one of the tan patio chairs. The cushions with their green, yellow, and white floral design were very comfortable and yet her body felt dissatisfied sitting on them. "Let's not act ignorant to our situation. You're still married, albeit separated." Which she still couldn't believe hadn't been rumored around the office. "I have a boyfriend."

"Who doesn't love you enough to marry you," he said when he'd come outside, taking a seat in the chair across from her, spreading his legs as he sat back and continued to watch her.

Because his words were too close to the truth they stung, Casey flinched. She closed her eyes and took a deep breath. "We work together. Very closely together. To our coworkers our 'attraction' might seem like a conflict."

"We work on the same team, Casey. There's no conflict."

"It's my idea that we're implementing into a half-million-dollar commercial tomorrow. My plans that won over Panzene and this account. That doesn't seem like a conflict to you? Or at the very least, favoritism on your part?"

"No," he answered simply. "It sounds like I know my job well enough to recognize talent. I knew when I interviewed you that you were smart and that you would produce fantastic, innovative ideas for the company and our clients. To date, you haven't let me down. Rest assured, Casey, no matter how beautiful you are, I wouldn't risk my name and reputation in the business world if I didn't trust you could do the job I hired you to do."

She opened her mouth to say something else and he raised a hand to stop her. "If you want to sit here all night and come up with reason after reason why our attraction could cause problems, go right ahead. But it won't make it go away. I can promise you that."

"What do you want from me?" she asked, exasperated by the way his legs had fallen open, his palms resting on his thighs, his muscled chest moving as he spoke.

"Come here."

She only stared for a moment, then when he raised a brow to her she stood slowly. Walking across the small patio toward him seemed like it took forever. When she stood directly in front of him, he sat forward, reached out and took both her hands in his.

With a slight tug he had her between his legs. He looked up, watching her even as his face moved closer until he was kissing her navel through the thin crushed cotton material of her dress.

"I want to make you happy," he whispered.

Casey gasped and tried to pull away. But the motion wasn't serious, as Bernard knew, so his hold on her didn't even have to increase to keep her in place.

His tongue extended and he continued kissing that spot until the dampness of the material felt cool against her skin.

"I want to make you scream with pleasure," he continued.

Her legs were trembling, threatening to give out on her at any moment. She bit her bottom lip and tried to keep her cool.

"Has anybody ever made you scream, Casey?" he asked, pushing her hands up to cup her own breasts.

Casey wasn't into masturbating. The only time she felt her body was when she washed. Simon was a good lover, he took care of her in that way. Still, the feel of her now heavy breasts in her palms was erotic and naughty and had her heating all over.

His hands were busily pushing her dress upward, his fingers hooking in the band of her thong, pulling it down her legs. "Answer me," he commanded in a voice so subtly sexy her pussy contracted with its tone.

"Nobody's ever made me scream," she whispered, hating the truth to her answer. Simon was good, but he wasn't *that* good.

"Look at me."

She opened her eyes and looked down into his face.

"You're going to scream my name." His fingers were griping her thighs, pulling them apart.

Casey wobbled as if she were about to fall. He clasped one hand to the base of her back to steady her.

"Loud and long, you're going to scream and come for me." With his other hand he slipped between her legs, using one finger to separate her pussy lips.

She opened her mouth but no sound came out. Everything was caught up in that one movement, that one finger that slid sinuously over her moistened folds, driving her steadily toward that peak of insanity.

"Only me, Casey." He stroked her cunt like an experienced guitarist, the tiny moans emanating from her throat a song he'd authored alone.

"You'll scream for only me."

As his stroking continued in that slow, deliberate motion, Casey began to take his words for what they were, the complete and absolute truth. So help her God.

Chapter 8

Bernard laid her on the lounge chair, loving the cool night breeze that brushed over them on the open patio. The thought that someone might see them held more appeal than he'd ever imagined.

It must be his surroundings. In his hours at Horizons he'd seen a bit more than the brochure had boasted. There was the open nudity that had taken him a bit by surprise. He still wondered how he really felt about that. In his mind there were some positions he didn't really want to see a naked woman in, like coughing when she choked on a drink that was too strong for her or squatting to pick up the hotel key card she'd dropped—wait a minute, that last one held some appeal.

But he didn't know these women. He hadn't been attracted to these women for two years. So despite what some considered the natural reaction for a man in the presence of naked women, Bernard had not been impressed. Instead, he'd found himself wondering if Casey would adhere to the au naturel code and strip for him.

Of course that wouldn't happen. Casey was too classy,

too subdued to walk the halls of this resort naked. She was uptight and confused and he . . . he was her savior.

That's exactly how Bernard thought of himself where Casey was concerned. She needed to get out of her dead-end relationship. She needed to release the passion he'd seen banked in her eyes. She needed to cum while he was buried deep inside of her, over and over again.

She was pliant beneath him, the mini-orgasm he'd brought her by simply stroking her pussy had relaxed her totally. So now she lay against the lounge, waiting, wanting. With slow motions Bernard lifted first one, then the other leg, hooking them on opposite arms of the lounge chair until her pussy was spread before him like a holiday feast.

Bernard, lowering himself to sit on the edge of the seat between her legs, had to adjust his dick to keep it from bursting through his zipper. She said she didn't want to have sex. Well, he didn't either. He wanted to fuck her senseless. But he wanted her to trust him more. So he wouldn't penetrate her tonight, not with his dick.

Using his thumbs, he separated her folds until her pussy was completely exposed from the cute little bud of her clit to the weeping entrance to her treasure. He could even see her puckered anus and felt his mouth water with anticipation.

She arched upward in the chair just as his thumbs moved over her clit.

"Bernard," she whispered.

He smiled. "You're going to say it louder than that. Soon."

With her spread wide Bernard dipped his head low and licked her long, slow, deep. Her essence coated his tongue and he swallowed, savoring the sweet taste he'd known would be there.

She grasped his head and he dipped low again, sucking her plump folds into his mouth then whipping his tongue up and down until she was writhing, her breath coming in quick pants. He began kissing her, intimately dueling his tongue with her pussy lips, her essence with his spittle. Inhaling and exhaling her scent had his dick near to bursting, until he had no other recourse but to slip two fingers inside her.

"Mmm, Bernard," she panted.

It still wasn't loud enough, he thought to himself, and began feverishly working his fingers inside of her. Her hips jutted forward, meeting the thrusts of his hand. With his other hand Bernard toyed with her clit all the while still licking her lavishly.

She was thrashing about on the brink of an orgasm that would definitely have her seeing stars, but it wasn't enough. Bernard wanted to claim her. On this first night here at this beautifully seductive resort he wanted her to think of only him, remember only him.

So while her clit was in his mouth, his fingers deep inside her pussy, Bernard moved his other hand further south. He touched her anus just briefly and felt her stiffen there.

Fantastic; his mind was exploding with glee. She wasn't used to being touched there. Her boyfriend didn't touch her there. She was an anal virgin and his for the taking.

Lightly he tapped the tips of his fingers to her tightened sphincter. She inhaled quickly, squeezing her ass cheeks in an effort to remove his hand.

"Don't deny me, Casey. Please, not this. Don't deny me this." His words seemed strained even to his own ears and when she relaxed he sighed her name, moving his mouth over her pussy once again.

His finger touched her tight hole, spreading the

essence of hers that dripped from her finger-fucked pussy. It was so slippery now that the touch of his finger went further, the tip going slowly into her.

She shivered and Bernard knew he'd hit the jackpot. Removing his finger, swirling it around, he then pushed back into the tight entrance once more, this time letting more of his finger slip inside.

"Fuck," she gasped and he pulled his mouth away from her pussy.

"Oh yeah, that's exactly what I'm going to do," he groaned then began a slow dance with his two fingers moving inside her pussy while his one finger backed out of her anus. Into her anus and out of her pussy. Back and forth, in and out. His hands were drenched as he looked down at her glistening pussy, her tight ass.

"Bernard," she whispered.

His motions continued, tortuously slow.

"Bernard." Her head shifted back and forth on the chair.

"Bernard!"

And that was it, the pitch he'd wanted. If there were anyone on the patio in the room to either side of hers they were sure to hear her. Hell, the people at the pool had probably heard her.

His motions picked up, just as his heart rate did. Damn, but he wanted to be inside her, he wanted to re-place either one of his fingers with his dick. But he had to remain in control. Had to give her what she needed in order to gain what he wanted.

So he continued working her until her body bowed up off the lounge and she screamed with the intensity of the orgasm overtaking her body.

She was beautiful as she yelled, her hair spread around her face like a dark halo, her pussy convulsing around his fingers, her ass tightening, pulling him in deeper.

When she'd crested he rose over her, stretched his

body out along hers and kissing her. Long, deep, sensuous. With the motions of his lips and tongue on hers he told Casey McKnight what he wanted from her, what he needed from her, what she would ultimately relinquish to only him.

And with a defeated sigh she wrapped her arms around his neck, knowing that from this moment on she'd give this man whatever he wanted, needed—to hell with the consequences.

"He's at it again."

Lisette held the phone to her ear, tears quickly springing to her eyes. She immediately stood and left the table, her father and Perry Sunder, his political strategist, staring after her, baffled.

"Who is this?" she whispered, going out onto the balcony of the Rusty Scupper restaurant where they were having dinner.

"If you don't do something about him, I will."

Then there was a click. She'd known the call wouldn't last long. This was the third one in as many weeks. The caller's number was always anonymous, his warnings spoken quickly, his voice obviously disguised but vaguely familiar. She hadn't told Nola about them because she wasn't sure how this might alter the plan they'd devised together.

Speaking of which, since she'd called Nola, attempting to back out of that plan, the woman hadn't called her back. She would call her in the morning, Lisette decided as she checked the caller ID on her phone, once more knowing that it would read *unknown number*.

So somebody else knew that her husband was a liar and a cheater, somebody else felt he needed to pay for his transgressions.

Unfortunately, Lisette wasn't so sure. She loved Ber-

nard, still. It sat like a rock in her chest, this bundle of
feelings she had for this man, the father of her child. She
couldn't let go that easily. She wouldn't give up her husband without a fight.

"You okay, princess?" Arnold Winston came up behind
her, wrapping an arm around his only child.

"I'm fine, Daddy," she said, resting her head on his
shoulder.

"Who was on the phone? The way you ran out I
thought something might be wrong with Madison."

"Oh, no. She's fine. Just ah . . . ah . . . Ananda just
wanted to tell me something."

Arnold's thick, bushy brows furrowed. "How's she
doing? I hear the divorce is getting messier."

"It is. I don't envy her at all." Lisette found a truth to
her words that she hadn't really considered before last
night, when Bernard had made love to her. This time had
seemed different, Bernard was more intense, focused on
pleasing her than he'd ever been before and she loved it.
The act meant all the more to her because of the way
he'd murmured over and over how much he'd needed
this—the lovemaking with her—she'd supposed. She'd
needed it too, as confirmation.

"Of course you don't. You and Bernard have a much
better marriage than that. I have big plans for my son-in-
law, plans that will see us all rich and happy."

If only he knew. With a frown, Lisette said, "We're already rich, Daddy."

Arnold tweaked her nose. "You can never be too rich.
Now come on back to dinner. I was just about to tell
Perry about Bernard and what an asset he'll be to the city
council."

Dutifully, Lisette followed, wondering what an asset
her husband was to her. It wasn't about money or pres-
tige or this career or that one, for her it was about one

thing and one thing only: keeping her family intact. She was determined to do just that, no matter how many times the nagging voice in her head said differently.

First thing tomorrow morning she would fire Nola Brentwood. The woman was vindictive and hell-bent on doing things her way, regardless of the fact that Lisette was the one paying her. At times it seemed as if Nola had a personal ax to grind. Well, either way, Lisette wasn't sure she wanted to be a pawn in the woman's game.

The minute Bernard returned from Antigua she planned to approach him about his infidelities and lay down some new ground rules. The cheating had to stop; she'd let it go for long enough. They would go to counseling if need be, to figure out where and when their relationship had gone wrong. They were both going to fight for this marriage, for the sake of their daughter.

Feeling liberated and focused, she took a deep breath and released it. She was doing the right thing. It was past time she took control of this situation and fought for the life she wanted.

Actually, it was past time you came to your senses and made that lying bastard pay for the way he's been treating you.

Lisette closed her eyes to the voice, the words that so often rang in her head. That wasn't how she wanted to handle this situation, it wasn't the way she wanted her life to go. The problem was, there were times when she didn't think she was strong enough to fight it.

Chapter 9

Meosha disconnected her cell phone just as Kingsley, aka Nola Brentwood, emerged from the shower.

Meosha had known she'd seen that woman somewhere before and once they'd come to her room after their earlier encounter she'd remembered. It had been in the local papers and the trial had even been featured on one of those crime and justice programs. Nola Brentwood was the woman who'd been played by her cousin's ex and shot his balls off in retaliation. Meosha couldn't remember all the names of the people involved or what had happened to the man with the missing balls or Nola's cousin, but what she did remember was the feeling of pride she'd felt upon hearing about the case. For once a woman had gotten revenge. Sure, there was that other woman who had sliced her cheating husband's dick off, but then she'd apologized afterward, which had made Meosha sick to her stomach.

Nola Brentwood had shot that man right in front of her cousin and walked away. Even at the trial she'd showed no remorse, which Meosha thought might have ended with her getting more jail time. But apparently Nola had good legal counsel and a female judge who could probably relate to the circumstances.

When they'd stood in her room, Meosha had felt a momentary slither of fear as she'd looked into the cool, dark eyes of Nola Brentwood and listened as the woman told her of the plan to bring Bernard Williamson and his lying, cheating ass down. The pride Meosha had originally felt when hearing about Nola Brentwood's trigger-finger exploits had swelled until Meosha felt compelled to do whatever Nola asked her to do.

So they'd gone to the dinner meeting, Meosha not revealing the fact that the Panzene rep was really a private investigator of sorts watching CCM's star exec as he ogled Casey McKnight.

A part of Meosha was still stung by Bernard's treatment of her, but now she had a new focus. If she helped Nola, she'd be paid well and after the shit hit the fan with Bernard and Casey, they would both be out of the company, which meant Meosha could move up on the food chain.

She didn't love Bernard Williamson, that much was true. Yet, she liked sleeping with him, liked the prospect of what being with him could bring her. She made it a point to never let her feelings get involved when she was with a man, it was just too complicated. So the fact that Bernard now wanted to end their affair and had so quickly moved on to someone else did two things: proved she was right not to let men into her heart and pissed her off royally. To the point that what Nola was offering her outweighed whatever physical feelings she'd had for Bernard.

"So what I'm thinking is that we need to set Bernard up," Nola was saying, effectively bringing Meosha back to the present. She sat on the bed, clad only in the thick, fluffy white towel provided by the resort. Lifting one long, golden-hued leg, she began to lotion her smooth skin.

Meosha swallowed and attempted to look nonchalant. She was not turned on by this woman.

"I don't think we'll have to do that, he's so open for Casey all we'd have to do is follow him with a camera and his ass would be caught."

Nola shook her head. "No. That's not enough. For what I have planned for him I need something deeper, something more scandalous then just a kiss or a grope in the hallway of a hotel. He can explain that away too easily."

She lifted her other leg and Meosha could swear she'd seen the lips of her pussy. Was it getting hot in here? No, of course not. Meosha didn't swing that way. She loved the dick too much to even consider getting her rocks off by licking some woman's pussy.

But Nola Brentwood wasn't some woman. She appealed to Meosha on a level that nobody ever had. Nola related to her and the mindsct she had against men. Not even her best friend, Kalita, could do that. Besides, Meosha liked Nola's style. Not just in the bomb-ass clothes she wore, or the chic and professional air she had about her, but in her sexuality.

The woman oozed confidence, even when she'd licked Meosha's ear and Meosha had tentatively felt her butt, she hadn't ruffled. She'd looked at Meosha as if the entire interlude had been a part of her plan. She hadn't even asked if she could come back to Meosha's room after the meeting, she'd simply followed her inside. And when she'd begun to undress, Meosha became tongue-tied. Now Nola was sitting on her bed, naked but for the towel and Meosha couldn't help but wonder what her buttery smooth skin would feel like beneath her fingers, her tongue. Wait a minute, hadn't she just reiterated to herself that she didn't swing this way? Maybe she was just overreacting. This woman couldn't possibly be coming on to her.

"Come here and sit down, Meosha," Nola said calmly, patting the side of the bed next to her.

Damn, had she caught her staring at her pussy? Did she somehow detect the distinctly naughty thoughts that were going through Meosha's head?

Well, Meosha was no amateur either, at least she wasn't going to act like one in front of Nola. So she moved confidently to the bed and sat down.

"You're down for this, right?" Nola asked.

Meosha looked at her closely before answering because she wasn't sure what aspect of their involvement the woman was referring to. "Bernard tried to dump me for Casey. I'm not going out like that."

Nola smiled, then reached out, touching a hand to Meosha's cheek. "You're very attractive, Meosha. I don't see why he'd dump you for her."

Shit. Shit. Shit. She'd answered the wrong question. Okay, she needed to calm her rapidly beating heart and act like the mature playa that she was. Licking her lips, she extended her arm inwardly, threatening her fingers if they dared shake before resting on Nola's bare knee.

"I think you're attractive too." To her own ears the words sounded a little immature so Meosha followed them by moving her hand from Nola's knee up her thigh.

Nola's smile widened. "We're going to work well together," she said then leaned a little closer to Meosha, her eyes trained on Meosha's lips.

"Yeah, Bernard isn't going to know what hit him."

"And you aren't going to know what hit you," Nola said seconds before touching her lips to Meosha's.

This was the first time Meosha had ever kissed a female but the instant Nola's tongue crept inside her mouth she knew she was going to enjoy it. The feather-light movement of Nola's tongue against hers had Meosha's nipples hardening. Nola moved slow enough for Meosha to back away if she wanted, but with enough persistence that Meosha knew she meant business.

Her hands, now very steady, lifted to grab the top of the towel covering Nola's body, pushing it down until the woman's pert breasts were cupped in her palms.

Fuck! This felt good. Meosha moved closer, pressing Nola for a deeper kiss as she toyed with her nipples. Then Nola pulled away, that sinister smile still on her pretty face. Meosha wanted to kiss her again, she wanted to fist her fingers in Nola's short-cropped hair, she wanted to lick her golden body all over.

"Get undressed," Nola instructed as she moved further up on the bed, resting against the pillows.

Meosha did as she was told, then climbed onto the bed with Nola. A small part of her was nervous and unsure of what she was doing with this woman she'd only met a few days ago; scared of the implications what she was about to do meant. She'd never been with a woman before. Truth be told, never even thought about it until now. Until Nola.

A bigger part, the curious, courageous part of her was hungry for more. So when Nola held her arms out to her Meosha climbed on top and fell into another blissfully erotic kiss.

"It should be a sin for a woman to be that fine," Leonard said his eyes fixated on Kingsley.

"You haven't hit that yet?" Bernard teased as they stepped out of the limo that had brought them to the first location site for the commercial.

They were at Rendezvous Bay, on the southwest coast of Antigua, where the beaches were less developed and so, less populated. With that said, the tropical beauty was still top-notch. The sky was a breathtaking sapphire blue dotted with minimal puffy white clouds, while the water boasted a clear turquoise color with pure white sand beaches.

"Have you hit Casey yet?" Leonard replied stiffly.

Bernard's head snapped in his friend's direction. His tone was different, but even through the dark shades Leonard wore, similar to the ones Bernard had on himself, Bernard knew the other man was giving him a knowing look. "Nah, but I'm working on it."

Leonard smiled, held out his fist for a dap and chuckled. "I hear ya, man. She is hot."

"Yeah. I'm thinking she might be a little more than that."

"What?" Leonard paused, then asked, "Like leave Lisette and marry her type of material?"

Bernard shrugged. "I don't know. Maybe."

"Are you sure about that?" Leonard questioned as they walked along the beach following behind the producer, Jay Wintro, Casey, Meosha, and Kingsley.

After his last tryst with Meosha and the brief times he'd spent with Casey, Bernard had for the first time considered that very option. But was he ready to give up what he had at home? He wasn't thrilled with Lisette, that was no secret. Not that she wasn't a beautiful and intelligent woman, she just didn't excite him physically anymore. He'd sort of slipped into the relationship with her and then with the arrival of Madison, slipped into the role of husband and father. Lately, he'd wanted nothing more than to slip right out the door.

The problem was the one female he loved above all others: Madison. The thought of not seeing her, not being with her on a daily basis, was intolerable. Both Bernard's parents had raised him, whether or not their relationship was a love match, he couldn't personally attest to. But what he did know was that nothing, absolutely nothing, came before their love for him. The last thing he wanted was to have to see Madison on court-selected days. He wanted her permanently, unconditionally and he was determined to give Madison that same upbringing his parents had given him.

Besides, it was his wife that he felt like he was finished with, not his duties as a father. On another front he also had to consider what leaving Lisette would do to his ultimate career goals. If they did divorce, Arnold would not be pleased. As such that would leave Bernard at CCM and not in politics. To make matters worse, Arnold was one of Corbin Censor's top consultants. The man almost didn't breathe without asking Arnold's thoughts first. So leaving Lisette would put both Bernard's career goals and his family creed in jeopardy.

"I think right here is good," Casey said, turning back to get Bernard's approval.

And once again the conflict inside him raged.

When their gazes locked it was with the intimate knowledge of last night and what was to come. She'd been so responsive to his touch after her first bout of uncertainty that Bernard knew from here on out seducing her would be a piece of cake. But he wasn't ready for the world to know that. So he turned away, acted as if he were looking out along the beach.

"What do you think, Jay?" he asked the producer. "That rise of rocks over there might overtake the shot a bit."

Jay was by his side in a minute. "Yeah, but if we position Georgette and Shai just right along here—" he was pointing just beneath the rise of rocks to a small grassy spot that met the white sand seamlessly—"we could get a good shot. We're focusing on the sunblock and facial products today."

"That's right, the natural look of the cosmetics while lying on the beach is what we're aiming for here."

"Got it. This spot will work fine." Jay motioned to a man that Bernard assumed was his assistant. "Bring the trailer around and tell Georgette and Shai we'll be ready in about twenty minutes."

"This is one sexy beach," Meosha said, coming up behind Bernard and rubbing a hand over the small of his back.

Bernard casually stepped out of her reach. "It is."

"Did you get the schedule of events for today at Horizons?" she asked with a coy smile.

"I did," he replied crisply.

"I was thinking of getting a sensual massage."

Meosha wore a canary yellow bikini, which glistened brightly against her mocha complexion. The top barely covered her dark chocolate nipples and tied at the base of her neck, while the thong bottom had one thin string trailing an alluring line that was quickly lost in the crevice of her bottom. She wore a sheer covering around her waist but Bernard couldn't figure out what the hell that was for, since it hid absolutely nothing. Then again, he'd seen all that she'd had to offer and was not really amused.

"We should wrap up fairly soon. I think we've only rented the beach until noon so you should have plenty of time to enjoy yourself at the resort."

"I'd enjoy myself even more if you joined me."

"No," he said simply. "I told you it was over."

"And I told you it wasn't."

"Look," he said, glaring down at her seriously. To get his point across he snatched his glasses off so she could see the intense glare of his eyes. "This is done. We had fun but we both knew the rules. When it's over, it's over.

Don't belittle yourself by trying to push for something more."

This dirty bastard! No, he was not talking to her as if she were some high school flunky with a crush on her teacher. She should scratch his pretty face right now, then tell his wife and whoever else would listen about all the raunchy things he'd done to her over the last few months. But she caught sight of Nola walking along the beach with Leonard steadily on her heels and took a deep breath.

They'd spent the night together and it was beyond anything Meosha could have ever imagined. She'd thought that Bernard was good at licking her pussy until she came but Nola definitely took the prize. Her thighs quivered with the thought. So she didn't need Bernard anymore. Still, his rebuff stung and she wasn't about to take that lying down.

"Don't trip. I'm not infatuated with you and I'm not looking for any type of commitment. But you should know that what went on between us isn't classified info. I know of at least one person who'd be interested in hearing about our little excursions." She smiled at the instant fury she saw brewing in his eyes.

"Don't fuck with me. You won't win," he told her, then stomped off.

From a distance, Nola watched her and when Meosha caught her gaze again the woman blew a kiss her way. Meosha caught the kiss and rubbed her finger over her lips, remembering just how hot Nola's touch had been.

Then Leonard touched a hand to Nola's waist and Meosha found herself wondering, what was going on there?

Chapter 10

Meet me in Suite 18 @ 2 pm
The note was cryptic at best, still Casey knew who it was from and what it meant.

A month ago Bernard Williamson was just her sexy-as-hell boss. A few days ago he'd kissed her, opening the door to an attraction she'd harbored but never planned to act on. And now, she found herself anxious to be alone with him.

It was beyond strange, considering her campaign for a marriage proposal from Simon, and yet to some degree Casey felt as if it were fate.

Simon wasn't on board with her plan for the future, and no ultimatum was going to put him there. And if it did, what did that mean to her ultimately? Did she really want a man she'd had to force to marry her? No, either he wanted her forever or he didn't. Simon's answer was resoundingly clear. She'd only had to push her feelings aside for a moment and really listen to him. He didn't want to marry her.

Did Bernard?

How could he, he was already married. That in and of itself should have been a big enough red flag to stop this physical pull she felt toward him. But it hadn't. Just as her parents' warnings and Pastor Edgerton's preaching hadn't stopped her from letting Tommy Edgerton kiss and fondle her while in the pulpit that Saturday afternoon. When Tommy had pulled her to the front of the church she'd followed behind him, giggling with the joy of the attention he was giving her. But when they took the two steps leading them from the altar to the pulpit, then continued until they were nestled behind the oak beams that ran along the front of the church, boxing in the chairs and the podium, she'd had second thoughts.

Just like the ones she was having now.

Casey had known what she and Tommy were about to do was wrong, and yet she hadn't stopped him.

Being with Bernard was wrong on so many levels. Still the warmth that pooled in her stomach, the heat that settled comfortably in her vagina when she thought of him, were steadily pushing those convictions aside.

Coming back from the beach, Casey had meant to ask Meosha about the true state of Bernard's marriage. Of course, it was probably out of line for the two women to discuss their boss's personal life but the fact that she hadn't heard about his separation at some time in the office was nagging at her.

Not enough to keep from seeing him, however. As she stepped out of the shower, Casey dried off with one of the fluffy towels and went to the dresser to retrieve her body oil. It was lightly scented, jasmine. She smiled as she checked the bottle; one of her favorite scents. As she covered her body with the enticing scent she thought of what lay in store for her in Suite 18.

*   *   *

"I haven't heard from her since earlier yesterday," Gee told Cameron Hunt, one of his longtime friends.

"You tried calling her?"

"Not getting any answer." They were in the gym, where Gee was bench-pressing three hundred pounds of steel without breaking a sweat. His insides clenched as he listened to the conversation he was having. Never in his life had he talked to one of his friends about a woman. Never had he been this stressed-out over a female.

But then, until a year ago, he'd never slept with a woman like Nola Brentwood.

To say she was everything he'd ever wanted in a woman was an understatement. She was all that and then some. And it wasn't just sex for him. Sure, he loved Nola's uninhibited sexual appetite, loved her eagerness to please him as well as her adamancy about being pleased herself.

Yet those were only small things compared to the big picture. She was gorgeous, intelligent, courageous, and spirited. She didn't focus her life on pleasing him, she had goals and she went after them. She wasn't codependent like a lot of the females he'd dated in the past.

And he was desperately in love with her.

"Maybe she wants to be left alone," Cam stated drily.

Gee dropped the bar with a loud clink and his friend looked at him quizzically.

"What? Man, I know you're not trippin' over some chick!"

"Watch your step," Gee warned.

"Me?" With a disgusted look and a shake of his head, he continued, "No, you need to watch yourself. You know these women are scandalous. You said you met her inside, she's scandalous *and* a criminal. I told you before about fucking with those inmates."

"She's not like that."

"Yeah, right. She was in for shooting a man's dick off

and you wanted to fuck her. That was plain crazy from the jump. Now you're all tied up in her and she's brushing your ass off. You need to find some new pussy and move on." Wasn't that what Cam had tried to do after the woman he thought he'd loved had set him up and sent him to jail?

"I don't want anybody else," Gee said almost solemnly.

Holding his sides with laughter, Cam took a quick step back as Gee lifted up from the bench. He wasn't totally out of his mind. Gee was a big dude and when he was pissed off, as dangerous as any human of 280 pounds who usually carried three guns on him at a time could be.

"I see. I see. You're in *love*," he said with great exaggeration.

Gee gritted his teeth, then leaned his neck to both sides until a resounding *crack* echoed in the loud gym. "I want you to watch her. If she's fucking somebody else . . . no, if she's even touching somebody else I want to know."

"You're serious?" he asked but already knew the answer. In fact, he knew better than anybody exactly what Gee was going through, but he wasn't about to tell his friend that.

Gee stood, his beefy muscles flexing, wearing only basketball shorts. "I'm deadly serious."

Chapter 11

"So Kinglsey, how long have you been working for Panzene?" Leonard asked as he lifted his arms to rest along the rim of the pool.

He was absolutely loving this resort. This afternoon he was in the pool, the one that centered the courtyard to the back of the facility. There was another heated pool on the inside but he'd wanted to be out in the sun, continuing to enjoy the gorgeous day.

Plus, he'd overheard Kingsley telling Shai that she'd be in the pool later. Apparently, the football superstar was sniffing around her just like Leonard was. However, Leonard intended to get first dibs.

Kingsley Mason was one fine-ass woman, Leonard thought as he continued to watch her treading water and blinking up at him with those dangerously intelligent eyes. Since the first day he'd met her in the office Leonard had been intrigued by her. Imagine his surprise when that same night he'd been watching one of those true-crime shows and came across the quick sketch of the Baltimore woman who'd decided to get a cheating man back by shooting his balls off. His assumption was that Nola Brentwood had needed a job and with a criminal record thus needed to reinvent herself.

Hell, he wasn't mad at her. There were things in his past that were better left there as well. So he'd vowed to play along with her little secret, as long as it suited his needs.

Right now, however, his needs were stretched upward in his swimming trunks, pulsating as she licked her lips and made her way closer to him.

"A couple of years," she said, answering his previous question with a smile.

When she was standing directly in front of him, the water dipping and diving just at her shoulder level since they were in the five-feet section of the pool, he brushed a finger over her forehead, moving aside the thick piece of her short hair that was plastered there.

She was a phenomenally beautiful woman, with an intensity to her demeanor that both intrigued and amazed him. Her eyes held secrets; her mouth, endless hours of pleasure, Leonard thought, which incited another throb from his aching cock. Still, she wasn't the woman he was in love with.

"You do a great job. I'm sure the execs are happy to have you working for them," he said, commenting on her knowledge of the Panzene products and her keen vision in the execution of the commercial.

Although he knew that she'd been an attorney in her former life, he was quick to admit that she had the marketing game down pat. Her vision for the product development was clear, her eye for detail and her air of authority resonated throughout the entire commercial shoot. With her and Casey there, Leonard felt like he and Bernard could almost take a hike.

"I'm happy there," she answered simply, as if business was the last thing she wanted to talk about.

She was so close to him that Leonard couldn't miss the implication. As with earlier when they'd walked along Rendezvous Bay and he'd gotten the vibe that she was open to taking things further with him, her look confirmed her willingness. This was what he needed to take his mind off a situation he had yet to figure out how to change, the woman he'd been unable to make fall in love with him.

Pushing thoughts of her to the back of his mind, Leonard tried to do what he always did, live for the moment. He slipped one hand into the water around Kingsley's waist, pulling her until her body was flush against his own.

She neither blinked in surprise nor jerked away. She wanted to be in his arms and more than likely his bed.

"You're happy at Panzene. Well, I think I know what can make you happier," he said, bending his head to nip his teeth along the line of her neck.

She moaned, then tilted her head further back, allowing him complete access to her throat.

Nola's plan to expose Bernard had taken a turn last night as she'd lain beside Meosha. Now, Nola prided herself on being strictly-dickly, but damn, that woman had a body that just would not quit. She supposed that meant she was bisexual, as opposed to being a outright lesbian. How that new title made her feel, Nola wasn't all that sure. Besides, Nola knew the score and she knew it well. This was her job. Meosha Cannon had been sleeping with Bernard. For all intents and purposes she could wrap her case up with Meosha's confession alone.

But the fact that Bernard was happily moving to the next woman in the office made Nola sick to her stomach.

So his downfall needed to be painful—very painful—to make the message clear.

And who better than his best friend to help her in that regard.

"You have something for me?" she asked, sliding one of her legs up his until it was hooked behind his back.

"Oh yeah," he groaned and licked her neck.

Nola was neither impressed nor aroused. But she was wet, courtesy of the pool water and the searing kiss she and Meosha had shared just before she'd left the woman with her next assignment.

Leonard seemed to be hung quite nicely, but his butt-kissing show-off work attitude had turned her off immediately. That and the fact that he'd automatically assumed, the first time they'd met, that she'd end up in his bed. Well, she would, but when it was all said and done, she'd bet a dollar to a dime he wouldn't want to run back to Bernard to brag about it.

Meosha was more than discontented. The commercial shoot had gone pretty much as planned, with Casey stepping up and taking charge while Bernard looked at her like she was a rack of ribs at a Memphis barbeque. By the time they'd finished for the day she'd been ready to kick his flirting ass.

But truth be told, that wasn't the only thing bothering Meosha. Nola, while sticking as close to Leonard as she possibly could, had shown some experience in the marketing department as well. Giving comments and adding her two cents here and there made her really look like a Panzene exec. Meosha figured she was the only one who knew that Kingsley Mason was a fake. Both women had shown her up this morning, leaving her on the sidelines with anger boiling recklessly in her system.

Wasn't this where she always ended up? On the outside looking in? Damn, she was tired of the tables always turning on her. She wanted so much more from life than this sideline seat. She wanted . . . right at this moment, Meosha wasn't quite sure.

Was it more time with Nola? Never before in Meosha's life had she been with a woman intimately. The stark memory of Nola's tongue parting her tender folds made Meosha wet all over again. It had been a divine enlightenment, the way Nola's soft lips moved so seductively over her moist ones. And when she pushed her fingers inside her weeping cunt, Meosha had screamed in ecstasy.

Still, the longing for Bernard had burned into her with just as much, if not more, persistence. There was nothing like dick, not even the best pussy-licking she'd ever experienced. Meosha would be the first to say she wasn't in love with Bernard; the man just wasn't worthy of those types of emotions. But she was in heavy-duty lust with him. And she needed him—on a strictly financial level.

The promotion she'd received since fucking Bernard had increased Meosha's salary by ten thousand dollars last year. This year she was looking for more. She had plans for her money, for her future, and being in bed with her boss was going to make those dreams come true.

All her life Meosha had struggled to get what she'd thought she deserved. Being the youngest in a family with barely enough money to feed them after the rent and other household bills had been paid had been tough. Wearing her sisters' hand-me-downs was the norm and as she got older, sleeping with the boyfriends they'd discarded and getting from them what she could.

Meosha was smart enough to know that there were different ways of getting ahead in this world. A person had to use what skills they had to do what needed to be done. Prostitutes had never made enough money to suit Meosha's needs, and she wasn't about to sleep with any willing man. There was a method to her madness, a plan to her accomplishing her dream. If that plan entailed her sexing rich men like crazy, then so be it. In her mind it was as good as any other job out there, but with better perks.

Bernard Williamson was supposed to put her ahead several years in her plan. Through his position at CCM and his relationship with his father-in-law he wanted to move into politics. Sleeping with a politician was definitely a lucrative opportunity. And Meosha hadn't wanted anyone to get in her way of success. Especially not Casey McKnight.

After the commercial shoot, Meosha hadn't even gone back to her room to shower and change. By the way that Bernard had been gawking at Casey she knew he'd want to get into her drawers the moment they were back at the resort. And she wasn't mistaken.

Just a few minutes ago she'd watched Bernard slip into one of the spa rooms. These rooms had to be reserved ahead of time on an hourly basis. Meosha knew this because she'd made it her business to know each and every amenity that Horizons offered. Inside the spa rooms were deep, jetted Jacuzzi tubs centered in the marbled floors. There was a patio door leading to yet another balcony with a continuous view of the island on one wall, and mirrors on the other. A fully stocked bar and a plasma television complete with any and every type of porn flick you could imagine were amenities as well. There was no doubt that the spa rooms were meant for endless hours of fucking and sucking.

As she watched the door close behind Casey it took everything in Meosha not to snatch the bitch by her hair and pull her out of there. Luckily, she had more class than that.

With purposeful strides she walked down to the front desk and pulled out her cell phone. Dialing the number, she watched as the tall, skinny white man answered the phone.

"Hello, this is Mrs. Bernard Williamson," Meosha said in her most polished voice. "I'm trying to reach my husband but he doesn't seem to be in his room. This is a family emergency. Could you page him or get someone to take him an urgent message?"

"Good afternoon, ma'am. Yes, most certainly. I will try and locate Mr. Williamson. Is there a callback number I can give him?"

Meosha almost giggled at the man's instantly concerned expression. This type of shit was way too easy.

"He has the number. Just tell him to call my cell," she instructed the clerk.

"I sure will, ma'am. I'll take care of this right away."

"Thank you."

Meosha hung up the phone with a smile. The clerk had an appointment book right on the front desk. He could turn a few pages and locate exactly who had reserved what rooms and services and he'd know where Bernard was. She walked happily back to her room, knowing that Bernard would be getting none of the prissy Casey McKnight's pussy today.

Chapter 12

Casey had just slipped into the tub when Bernard's hands slipped around her waist, pulling her until she straddled his lap.

"I've been waiting all day to get my hands on you," he said, burying his face in the crook of her neck. He licked her skin then nipped her with his teeth, only to soothe the spot with his tongue once more.

Despite the warm temperature of the water, Casey shivered. "You were supposed to be concentrating on work this morning, not on me."

One of his hands cupped her ass while the other crept upward to grasp the nape of her neck. "What can I say? You're a distraction."

At his words, Casey stiffened a bit. Bernard paused as well, then refrained from kissing her neck and looked at her. "A very pleasurable one at that," he added, then kissed her lips with a fevered urgency that had her twisting in his arms.

Reflexively she ground her scarcely covered pussy into his pulsating erection. He wore swim trunks but from the feel of him she could tell he was itching to be free of them. So without further preamble Casey slipped her hands between them, reached past the elastic band of his trunks and found his waiting dick.

Bernard sucked in a breath as she held his thickness in her hands. She flexed her fingers until she had a good grip on his girth and pulled upward from the base. He groaned and she stroked him long and slow once more.

"Damn, I want to fuck you," he groaned.

His words were guttural, candid, and insatiably erotic. The candlelit room was as far as romance was going today. The message was clear: They were here to fuck, finally.

Slipping his hand around from her ass, Bernard pushed the thin wisp of material that represented the bottom of her bikini out of the way to thrust a finger into her pussy. She bucked and bit her bottom lip, squeezing the tip of his dick between her clenched fist during the process.

"It's going to be so good, Casey. So fucking good." He was thrusting his finger inside her pussy while his hips lifted from the bench in the tub. Casey's hands moved frantically over his dick as she pumped back against his hand. His words rang in her ears and she couldn't help but believe him. If their attraction was this intense, their foreplay this hot, then their final joining would be nothing short of combustible.

"Bernard," she whispered his name, wanting him inside her desperately.

"Tell me what you want, baby," he encouraged.

She sighed. "You," came a ragged pant as his finger worked frantically against her G-spot. "I want you."

"Yeah?" He pulled one finger out and replaced it with two. "You want me to do what?"

She didn't speak. Couldn't, actually, but wasn't ready to admit that to him.

"You want me to fuck that sweet pussy, Casey?" He continued to pump his fingers into her as she jerked his dick in what should have been painful motions.

"Huh? I can't hear you. Tell me to fuck that sweet, wet pussy." He leaned forward and bit her nipple.

Yes, he bit it. Not a gentle nipping with his teeth, then a brush with his tongue, but a full-fledged bite that sent tingles of pain that dissipated into pleasure up and down her spine.

"Yes!" she heard a voice scream and was amazed that it was her own. "Yes! I want you to fuck this pussy. Now!"

He chuckled, then grabbed her by the hips, lifting her up while he pushed his trunks down his thighs and off his feet. Casey didn't waste another minute. She pushed her thong down and watched as it floated beside his trunks in the bubbling water.

"Come here," he summoned her and she returned to his lap, her thighs quivering with anticipation.

She felt the broad head of his dick at her entrance and wondered if he'd fit. Before she had a chance to think any further, Bernard was grabbing her ass cheeks, parting them roughly as he lowered her pussy onto his dick.

His tip stretched her and she moaned. She wanted him to go slow, to not hurt her. But her body craved this, had been since the day she'd first met him, if she were totally honest. With that admission, she wanted to slam down onto his dick and let her body explode with pleasure all around him.

She flexed her hips, trying to take more of him in.

"Yeah, you want this dick, don't you?" he asked.

"Yes. Yes. I want it."

And damn, he was going to give it to her. The realization that he was finally fucking Casey ran through

Bernard's brain like a locomotive. He thrust his hips upward and felt her walls stretching around him. She was
tight, sweetly tight, for a woman with a boyfriend. But
Bernard quickly pushed that last part out of his mind.
From this moment on she was his and only his. He was
going to mark this pussy so that Simon or no other man
could ever fuck her the same again.

"Bernard," she whispered his name and his entire
body melted into hers. His dick was only halfway im-
paled in her and he needed more. He needed to be deep,
deep inside her, to cum in the warm depths of her pussy,
to hear her say his name once more.

Instead what he heard was a quick rapping at the door.
He opted to ignore it, pushing deeper into Casey's cunt.
There was another knock, then his cell phone started to
ring.

"Fuck!" he yelled.

Casey froze above him, then stared at the door with
blurry, aroused eyes. "Someone's at the door?" she asked,
not sure if she were hearing things or if there was actually someone interrupting them.

The knock persisted and then there was a hushed request. "Mr. Williamson? Sir? I have an urgent message for
you."

"Dammit!" Bernard cursed again. "Write it down and
slip it under the door," he told the person on the other
side.

"It's really important," came the reply.

Casey was already pulling away from him, lifting her
hips until his dick slipped right out of her. The loss was
quick and she wavered slightly in the still jetting water.
"You should go, get the message, I mean."

"No. This is our time," he said, reaching for her but she
was already across the tub retrieving the bottom to her
suit.

"It might be Mr. Censor or something about the commercial," she said, slipping into the rest of her suit. The interruption might be about work, or it might be about his family. Because unlike her, Bernard did have a family. Being separated from his wife didn't change that fact.

She was stepping out of the tub when she heard him curse again.

"Just wait a second, I'll be right there," he yelled to the door.

Casey heard the splashing of water as she went to the lounge near the mirrored wall and retrieved a towel. She didn't turn to see Bernard but knew he was putting on his trunks and getting out of the tub as well.

She felt strange as she heard him open the door, then curse again. Still she didn't turn, didn't want to know what the emergency was. Because something deep inside told her that it wasn't work-related and it wasn't good.

"Casey," she heard him say and her entire body went stiff.

He touched a hand to her shoulder. She didn't need to turn, only look up and she could see him staring at her through their reflection in the mirror.

"I have to go. It's an emergency at home."

"With your wife," she said in a tiny voice.

"With my daughter," he replied and for a moment Casey felt a small wave of relief. His daughter, not his wife. That was a relief. Or was it?

Was this what she had to look for by having an affair with a married man? Interruptions and priorities that didn't concern her? She saw herself nodding but knew she didn't understand. How could she when the family he was running out on her for was the same family she'd wanted with Simon?

Yes, Simon, the man she'd been in love with and sleeping with for the past five years. The man she was now cheating on.

Her head whirled with thoughts, recriminations, and regrets. Yes, Bernard needed to leave and she needed to get herself together.

Simon didn't want to marry her and Bernard couldn't marry her. So why the hell was she bothering with either of them?

"Go," she said simply.

"You can wait here. Enjoy the tub and I'll come back."

She was already shaking her head. "No. I'll go back to my room."

"Then I'll come there after I take care of this."

"No," she said adamantly and saw him flinch.

She didn't want to alienate her boss, even if she had no clue what she was doing with him or how this would ultimately affect her career. So she turned to him. "Take your time. Handle your business and I'll see you later tonight."

"Dinner?" he asked, sounding hopeful as his hand cupped her cheek.

"Kinglsey, Meosha, and I are already having dinner. We can meet up afterward."

She thought she saw a flicker of anger in Bernard's eyes but it quickly vanished, to be replaced by that sultry smile of his. "Okay. Join me in my room for a nightcap and some lovin'."

He kissed her lips lightly at first, then slipped his tongue into her mouth for an erotic duel of sorts. Casey wasn't entirely a fool. She'd join him in his room for some hot, sure-to-be satisfying sex. But it would not be lovin', because there was no love between her and Bernard. There was nothing but this.

She moaned and sank into the kiss, letting his tongue

openly explore her mouth, to twist and turn with her tongue, to engage her senses once more.

"Tonight," he whispered as he pulled away from her.

"Tonight," she echoed, already knowing how this would end.

Nola loved her job, all aspects of it, even—to her surprise—the lengths she had to go to keep the charade going.

She was back in her room after the morning's commercial shoot. In her mind things had gone only passably well. That's why she had papers spread all over her bed, proposals, pictures, reports, all pertaining to the Seduction line. While Nola had never entertained going into marketing, she couldn't ignore the ideas she'd had for Panzene's newest line.

The products were good, the angle fresh and still untapped enough in the commercial industry that they could take the lead. All-natural makeup had been around for a while, but the exclusive combinations that Panzene had come up with, resulting in fantastic products, was a veritable gold mine. But she wasn't sure the commercial was going to capture all that.

So she was thinking of a way to really spotlight Panzene's originality when her cell phone chirped. Enthralled in her work, Nola didn't even look at the caller ID, just flipped the phone open and answered.

"Girl, how long are you going to be in the Islands?" Cally's chipper voice resonated through the other end.

Two months younger than Nola, Cally was also Nola's polar opposite. She was cheerful and easygoing, smart and ambitious in a laid-back sort of way. Cally worked as a freelance writer and often put Nola in mind of the creative-artsy type. And Nola loved her like a sister instead of a cousin.

Today, Nola had no idea what type of happy juice Cally was sipping but she didn't really feel like the chitchat right now. Her mind had been shifting a lot lately. From this job and the ultimate breakdown of Bernard Williamson to her strange attraction to Meosha and right back to Gee and his high-handedness when it came to wanting a relationship.

Nola did not want a relationship. She never had. Her cousin Cally had said the same thing more than a year ago and look at her now. Still living with the good doctor Steven and now wearing the mammoth diamond he'd given her on Valentine's Day. So Cally would be the next cousin to get married.

Serena had already fallen, tying the knot just three weeks after Nola had gotten out of jail, with none other than her high school sweetheart. But Nola had always known Serena would fall, it was her nature. Serena was the youngest of the three cousins by four months total. Their mothers had been pregnant at the same time and loved every minute of it. Her parents had been happily married for longer than Nola could remember. It stood to reason Serena would reach for the same lifestyle.

Like Cally, Serena felt like Nola's sister and for that reason alone, Nola had come right home to dress fittings, spa treatments, and a host of other maid of honor duties that she didn't really care for, but did because it made Serena happy.

All in all, Nola was very pleased for her cousins. They'd found some sort of contentment in their lives and for that she was pleased. When her own contentment would come—because Nola was no fool and she didn't get hung up on the "happiness" bullshit—she had no idea.

"In another day or so. My part in this commercial was supposed to be minimal."

"Supposed to be?" Serena chimed in.

The cousins were known for their conference calls since each of them had really busy lifestyles.

"Yeah, I got kind of caught up in all the marketing bullshit earlier today. But you know that's not for me."

"Why? You've got a great business mind," Cally added. "Just look what you've done with your own company."

Serena chuckled. "She's hunting down men and threatening to bust their balls the same way she did Drew's, you call that a good business plan?"

"Sounds good to me," Nola chirped.

"That's not all she's doing. She's trying to make a statement and I'm proud of her for doing something that every woman has thought about at one point or another," Cally championed. "I'd like her to be a little more careful though, because some of these disgruntled men might get together and try to exact some of their own revenge on her."

"I wish the hell they would," Nola said, her mind already on the two guns she used to own legally and the ones she owned not so legally. She wasn't about to be anybody's fool again. She would protect herself and the people she cared for with everything she had.

"So have you almost got this guy caught?" Cally asked.

"He's so dumb he's about to walk right into my trap with his zipper open and his dick hanging out."

The threesome laughed.

"Men really are led by the wrong head," Serena chimed in.

"I know you're not talking about you're precious James," Nola said, bringing up the man who had once broken Serena's heart but now warmed her bed.

"No. James knows what to do and when to do it. My baby is always on point."

"Even when he's bringing that woman into your bedroom." The fact that James had initiated a threesome the moment he'd returned to Baltimore and to Serena's life was well-known between the cousins.

"Who? Sherry? Girl, she's just an incentive. James and I both enjoy her."

"Have you had her by yourself yet?" Nola couldn't help but ask. Since her little dip into the bisexual world she'd never had a woman with a man in the room. Nola liked way too much control to allow some dick in the same bed with her pussy. There was definitely no mixing and matching in her bedroom.

"Nope. And I don't want to."

"Has she had James alone?" Cally asked.

"Hell no!" Serena screamed.

"Okay, calm the hell down," Cally said, laughing. "I was just asking."

"She doesn't know what or who James has had when he's not with her." The moment the words left Nola's lips she regretted them. Just because she was distrustful and almost hateful on the male race, didn't mean that her cousin couldn't have a good relationship with her husband.

"Don't even go there. James and I have a very open relationship, so there's no need for any type of betrayal."

"Betrayal doesn't pick a certain time," Nola said. "But I take my statement back. James loves you and you've loved him for so damned long it's sickening."

"Well, I need to know when you're coming back so we can go get fitted for dresses," Cally interrupted.

"Dresses? For what?" Nola sighed. "Oh, no. No. No. No. I'm not going from dress shop to dress shop looking for another satin confection to walk down the aisle and stand next to another cousin determined to will their lives away with two simple-ass words." In this regard Nola was dead serious. Once Cally was married the entire dynamic of the threesome would be over.

It had never been a question that Serena would get married, she just had that nesting instinct. But Cally— Nola had always considered her and Cally kindred spirits, so once Cally was married, Nola would consider herself totally alone.

"We've set the date for August fifteenth. That gives me a little less than two months to get this planned and done," Cally was saying. "Nothing as formal as Serena had. Just a simple cocktail dress."

"But you've got to have flowers and a videographer."

"No flowers," Cally said. "Steven gives me enough flowers to start my own greenhouse. I'm not about to fill up a church with them too. I want it short and sweet, simple yet elegant."

"Borderline tacky," Serena grumbled.

"Now you know that is not in my repertoire. It'll be fabulous. So when are you coming back, Nola, to help me keep this simple affair from being taken over by the family females intent on making it a three-hundred-person spectacle?"

Nola couldn't help but laugh. She loved these two women more than anyone else in the world. There was nothing she wouldn't do for them, absolutely nothing. That's why she finally said, "I'll be home by the end of the week. We can have girls' night out at my place. You two spend the night and we can hit the stores first thing Saturday morning. How does that sound?"

"It sounds like I better give James enough tonight, tomorrow, and Friday morning so he won't be moaning and crying about me spending a night out."

They laughed and talked a few more minutes before disconnecting.

When Nola finally placed her cell phone on the nightstand next to the bed it was almost eight o'clock. She fell back on the bed, dropping an arm over her forehead.

She was having dinner with Meosha and Casey tonight. All a part of her plan. She wanted to see the two Williamson mistresses together to get an idea of what the man saw in each woman. She had a pretty good idea what he saw in Meosha, what every man with eyes saw— big tits and ass available for the taking. But Casey was slightly different. She didn't openly solicit men and gave the impression that the man who caught her put in a lot of work beforehand. So how long had Bernard been working on Casey? And had he finally caught her? Something told her there was still some distance between those two. Although they shared a lot of secret looks, they weren't the looks of longtime lovers. It was more the look of anticipation, of new arousal, of unchartered waters.

Well, after tonight, Bernard would think twice about venturing out into foreign waters altogether. She just hoped the brother could swim, because the sea of trouble he was about to find himself in would either make him a better man or kill him.

Nola and her cynical nature were betting on the latter.

Chapter 13

Leonard leaned against the wall, watching as Bernard fumbled with his key card. After a few unsuccessful tries Leonard felt sorry for his friend and took the card from his shaky fingers.

"At the rate you're going we'll be here all night," he said, then opened the door and pushed Bernard inside.

It hadn't been easy getting his friend drunk. Bernard was a man who liked to have all his senses about him at all times. But the moment Leonard started talking about Casey he'd watched Bernard go from the together businessmanhe'd always respected him as, to the simpering foolishness of a man whipped by pussy. Or in Bernard's case, whipped by the idea of pussy.

That's what was really sickening, his man hadn't even gotten a piece of that ass yet and he was all turned out. That's what made what Kingsley, Nola, had asked him to do much easier. She was trying to trap Bernard, to get the goods on him so that Lisette would have the upper hand.

Now to some that would make Leonard a sellout, ratting his friend's infidelities to his wife. But this wasn't the first time. Hadn't he just called Lisette last night to give her a heads-up about what her husband was doing on this little business trip? So as Leonard saw it, he was now looking out for his own interests. Helping Nola was going to help him in the long run. Lisette was too good for Bernard, too good for the way he treated her. Hopefully, Leonard's actions tonight would give her the freedom and respect she deserved and would open her eyes to the man who really loved her.

"I'm cool, man. I don't need you to tuck me in," Bernard said, every other word slurring with his sluggish movements.

"Good, 'cuz I'm not about to tuck your ass in. I just wanted to make sure you didn't fall on your face in the hallway. Mr. Censor wouldn't like that type of publicity coming from his key man."

Yeah, Bernard was the key man at the company, the go-to whenever there was a big account they definitely wanted to clinch. And yet he hadn't done anything that Leonard himself couldn't have done if given the chance.

"I'm just goin' sit her for a minute," Bernard said, plopping down on the end of the bed.

Leonard walked past and gave his right shoulder a slight push. "Go to sleep."

Bernard fell on the bed and Leonard walked toward the door. Opening it, he turned back and looked at what he would call his closest friend in the world. He shook his head. Bernard had no idea what was about to happen to him.

Leonard didn't feel a moment's guilt. Everybody who did dirt eventually got what they deserved.

He'd learned that lesson himself the hard way.

Getting the key pass to Bernard's room had cost Meosha a simple blow job in the employees-only office just beyond the front desk. Jeffrey, the tall, skinny white man who'd so graciously given her urgent message to Bernard, quite simply deserved it. And despite what some women thought about slim white dudes, Jeffrey was definitely packing. It was a most enjoyable experience with a payoff that could not be beat.

Slipping the card into the slot, she watched with anticipation as the light blinked green. Her hand was already on the handle and it clicked as she turned it to enter the room.

Nola was right behind her.

Once inside, Nola immediately began setting up her equipment. Nola's plan was to videotape their tryst to use for leverage with Bernard. Meosha's plan was a little more detailed. She wanted Bernard one last time. She wanted to taste his dick, to feel him inside her, then she wanted her own revenge. Nola had promised her a copy of the video for her own use. And Meosha planned to use it well.

They moved about in the dimly-lit room quietly until Nola pushed open the patio door. When Meosha turned to question her, the simple response was, "It's about to get real hot in here."

With that and a salacious smile, Meosha stripped off the short sundress she'd worn for this occasion. Beneath it she was naked, so she immediately moved toward the bed. Bernard was stretched out fully clothed on top of the sheets, his mouth slightly open as a soft snore escaped his lips.

She went for his shirt first, unbuttoning the light linen and slipping it off his arms until his chest was completely bare. Leaning forward, she kissed each nipple and felt her pussy lips tingle. If he wasn't such a bastard she could probably love this man. Probably.

Nola was at his feet, removing his shoes, socks, and then his pants. Meosha was too busy admiring his body or lost in her own world. Whatever, Nola didn't give a good goddamn. She was ready to leave this island town and all this drama. Cheating men, whorish women desperate to get ahead and naive women who didn't know when they were being played, got old with her real quick. Besides, she was feeling a little homesick and a lot confused about her personal life. So the sooner she got this part of her job over with, the better.

Now Bernard was naked, his impressive dick rising quickly to the occasion. Meosha grabbed hold of him first but Nola swatted her hand away.

"Remember the camera." Nola moved to the bedside table and flicked on the lamp. They needed extra light for the video to work. "Your face needs to be clear as well as his," she told the amateur. Nola didn't really know what she was going to do with Meosha after this. For as much as she was attracted to her she didn't trust the little slut as far as she could throw her.

Promising her one of the tapes was most likely a mistake but a small price to pay for her assistance. Unlike herself, Nola didn't think Meosha had what it took to exact revenge and walk away. Despite the woman's outward bravado, Nola could tell she'd let some personal feelings get involved. She could see it clearly in the way Meosha looked at Bernard. And that was a shame. She'd never make it trying to play men if she fell for them in the process.

Besides, just like the other men, Bernard wasn't going

to take blackmail lightly. She doubted if he was even going to take the scare tactic too pleasantly and give Lisette what she wanted—which, coincidentally, Nola wasn't even sure of anymore. Mrs. Williamson hadn't called her in the last day or so. The woman seemed to shift any way the wind blew with her decision of how to handle the tattered state of her marriage. As far as Nola knew the woman could have really changed her mind about taking her husband down, which was a damned pity. Still, Nola had to consider her reputation and the business she had worked hard to build. If Lisette wanted to back out she would probably have no other choice but to honor the woman's decision. No matter how much she abhorred it.

Sucking in a deep breath and pushing thoughts of Gee to the back of her mind, Nola stripped off the shorts and tank top she'd worn and climbed on the bed. Despite her stance against entering into a relationship she hadn't fucked another man in the year she'd been sleeping with Gee. What did that mean?

Absolutely nothing, she promised herself and went to work, propping Bernard's head up on the pillows. Meosha was between the man's legs again, taking his long dick into her mouth with expertise. For a minute Nola just watched.

Meosha's dark fingers circled his lighter toned dick. She jerked him upward then flicked her tongue over his smooth head. Pre-cum oozed from his slit and Meosha quickly lapped it up. Letting her hand slip to his base, she opened her mouth over him, swallowing his entire length.

Nola was impressed and vaguely turned on. She watched for a few seconds more as Meosha began to play with his balls, sucking them as if they were jawbreakers into her mouth.

Beneath her, Bernard moaned, his fingers instinctively clenching the sheets on the bed. Nola looked up one last time at the camera she'd planted, checking to be sure the red light was flashing, indicating the tape was rolling. When that was confirmed she scooted closer to him, touched his cheek as lovingly as she could pretend and turned his face toward her.

He was one handsome man whose looks and money had definitely precipitated the trouble he was now in. Still, he should have known better. He should have been loyal to his wife and to his daughter. He should have cherished them for the gift they were.

This wasn't a part of her original plan to take him down, but when she'd run into Meosha she'd had to improvise. Sure, she could have just let Meosha seduce the very intoxicated Bernard once more and catch it on tape, but Lisette was liable to let that slide. Putting herself in the mix was new for Nola and she wasn't real sure how she'd feel about it in the morning. But Nola had never been one for regrets. The end justified the means, she reminded herself.

The palm of her hand warmed and Nola found herself wanting to slap him more than seduce him. But that wasn't what she was being paid for. So with her other hand she lifted her medium-sized breast and spoon-fed him her dark nipple. He was just like a baby, opening his mouth as soon as he felt the tight nub glide over his lips. His body was in full response mode now as he reached up a hand and cupped her tit, taking her nipple between his teeth and biting down.

A shiver went down her spine and God help her she moaned, her head falling back slowly, her tongue stroking her bottom lip as ripples of pleasure spiked inside her.

Through the haze of desire she remembered this was

her job, this was what she was being paid to do. It was not who she was or what she intended to be. But then Nola never believed in dreams or fairy tales or happily-ever-afters. This was the hand she'd been dealt and with a moan of ecstasy she let her head fall back and resigned herself to play that hand as if it were her last.

Chapter 14

"When are you coming home?" Arnold Winston asked in an unusually brisk tone.

Bernard frowned into the phone and tightened the towel around his waist. He'd just awakened about a half hour ago. His bed looked like he'd had a rough night, pillows on the floor, sheets ripped off the mattress. His head hurt like hell and he was still trying to figure out why his chest, stomach, and thighs had been so sticky when he'd awakened. More importantly, he didn't remember taking his clothes off yet he'd awakened completely naked.

The last thing he needed was this wake-up call from his father-in-law.

"They were doing some shooting last night and then we have some time scheduled for this morning. Probably Friday evening. Why? What's the matter?"

Maybe this had to do with the urgent message he'd received yesterday, when he'd had to leave sweet Casey in the spa room. He'd called Lisette the moment he was back in his room but she hadn't answered. Another call to their nanny confirmed that Madison was okay, so Bernard had simply left a message on Lisette's cell phone and went on about his day. Since the tryst with Casey was shot he'd spent some time with the producer streamlining the production schedule so that he'd have more free time to spend with Casey before leaving the island.

"I need you back tomorrow," Arnold insisted.

"For what?"

"Perry's set up a meeting with the mayor. I think we've got a shot for next year's run."

For the millionth time in the past two days Bernard thought of why it was so important for him to take the seat on the city council instead of Arnold himself. But as he had in recent years, he remained silent.

"I don't know that I can make that happen," he answered, thinking solely of Casey. His free hand roamed over his bare abs and with the touch a flicker of memory flashed in his mind.

A hand had caressed him there, lips had kissed him there before moving steadily downward. Her hair was soft as he buried his fingers in it, pushing her lower, lower. Her mouth had been hot and moist as it covered the tip of his dick. Beneath the towel an erection swelled and Bernard struggled to keep his composure during the phone call with his father-in-law.

"Make it happen."

"Arnold, can't we set this up for Saturday night? I'll definitely be back by then."

"That's not the date I told you," he snapped. "Look, I'm putting in a lot of time and effort to get you into city hall. You'd think you'd be more appreciative."

"I don't recall asking you to put forth this time and effort," Bernard replied.

"I do what I do for my daughter and my granddaughter, to secure their future. I thought you understood that."

"I take good care of my family, Arnold." Even if he was contemplating leaving his wife.

"Let's not get into that."

"What's that supposed to mean?" Bernard asked, his temper growing with every word.

"It means that you are in a nonnegotiable position. Don't forget that I advise Censor or who to hire and fire in his firm. Now, you're either playing this my way or your ass will be unemployed and homeless. Got it?"

No, he didn't get it. Why was it so important for him to go to city hall? How did Arnold benefit?

Bernard did not take threats well and he wasn't about to start now. There was definitely something going on, a reason why Arnold wanted him in city hall so badly. A reason that Bernard was bound and determined to find out. Still, he hadn't gotten this far in business and in life without knowing when to play his hand close to the chest.

So taking a deep breath and expelling it slowly, he said, "I'll make arrangements to be there tomorrow night. Not for dinner but maybe late drinks or something. See what you can do. If not, it'll have to wait."

Disconnecting with his father-in-law, Bernard stood for a moment closing his eyes, trying to recapture the memory he'd just had. It was too real to be part of any dream. He could still actually feel the hands rolling over him, the mouth, the tongue, the heat infused through his entire body. Then with a start he remembered that Casey was supposed to meet him in his room at ten.

Had she come to his room? Had she been the one to touch him, to kiss him, to suck him off so expertly? He moved to the bed, taking a seat on the side and dropped his head to his hands, trying valiantly to conjure any other memories from last night.

His entire body tensed as he recalled sucking on pert nipples, tasting the sweet honey texture of pussy against his lips, feeling tight walls closing around his dick. He moaned with the sensations and cringed at the thought that Casey had come to him. He'd finally fucked her and now was barely remembering it all.

This is it. The job was done, Nola thought as she closed her suitcase and zipped it shut. Her flight was leaving in an hour and the clerk at the front desk had already called her a cab. She was going home.

A glance at her cell phone signaled that Gee had called once again. What was she going to do about him? She still wasn't sure. What could she do? Sleeping with Gee was unlike sleeping with any other man she'd ever been with before. But she didn't love him and she didn't want to marry him. Of that, she was almost positive. The fact that Cally was about to give in and finally marry her doctor was rubbing Nola the wrong way. Her temples throbbed and she felt sick to her stomach at the thought of what she'd done last night.

Not because she set a man up, because in her book Bernard Williamson was no man. She could care less what happened to him as a result of her careful ministrations. And truth be told, she wasn't really worried about what would happen to Meosha when all this hit the fan either. Meosha Cannon was definitely a woman used to taking care of herself. She would land on her feet, of that, Nola was absolutely sure.

Lisette, on the other hand, who had taken years to finally accept that her husband was cheating on her, and who was, even now, after hiring Nola and paying her hefty deposit, still wavering on whether or not to give this man what he deserved.

As a part of their original plan, Nola would approach

Bernard via e-mail or telephone, whichever was her choice, telling him of what she knew and demanding what Lisette wanted. Originally, Lisette had only requested he remove his name from Madison's trust fund and leave all of the joint accounts with the balances currently in them. Nola had laughed at that thought and added her own incentives.

Williamson was going to pay a hefty settlement to Lisette right off the bat. He was going to get off the trust account, leave the money in the other bank accounts and remove his name, fire Meosha and now Casey for being stupid enough to sleep with the boss, and publicly admit that the demise of their marriage was his fault and his fault alone. It wasn't really necessary for him to admit that he'd been a low-life cheating bastard. Most people with ten cents' worth of brains would figure that out for themselves. But Lisette's reputation was important to her. Her marriage was important, her success at being a mother and a wife. So for Bernard to publicly proclaim that the marriage had ended due to no fault of Lisette, Nola had no doubt would go a long way.

Bernard would either accept or decline her conditions. In the event that he accepted, things would go smoothly. In the event that he declined, then Nola would have to step up her game and really hit him where it hurt.

That thought alone made her shiver, because ruining other people's lives wasn't exactly what she'd set out to do. Still, she understood that there were always casualties in war. This time, they all rested on Bernard's shoulders.

An hour later Nola was on the plane waiting for it to take off, ready to be home again.

Chapter 15

The next two days passed in a blur. Bernard had returned to Baltimore on Thursday as he'd told his father-in-law he would. Part of the reason he was there on time and no doubt with a very surly attitude was because he hadn't seen Casey the last day and a half he was in Antigua.

After remembering more of their evening together he'd immediately gone to her room on Tuesday morning, only to find that she'd moved to another room within the resort. His first attempt to find out what room that was had been stalled by an emergency Leonard had with the commercial. The Panzene rep wanted a change in the location of the last part of the commercial and Leonard seemed hell-bent on making it happen. So they'd had to regroup, meet with the staff to map out the new direction and drive to a farther end of the island where Kingsley was convinced the lighting would enhance the look of the product on Georgette.

That had taken all of Tuesday and spilled over into Wednesday. So for the better part of Wednesday afternoon they'd been with the producer on the set with Shai and Georgette, trying to shoot the end of the commercial. Casey was not there. And neither was Kingsley, which upset Leonard but didn't bother Bernard either way. Bernard sensed Leonard had slept with the enticing Kingsley but didn't bother to ask since his own rendezvous had been stalled.

For the second night in a row he'd gone to bed without seeing or talking to Casey. He had, however, received a call from Lisette.

"So what was the emergency the other day?" he'd asked as soon as he'd realized it was her on the phone.

"There was no emergency," she answered. "Why would you ask that?"

Bernard was tired and irritated about the Casey situation as well as her father's high-handed dealing in his life, so he was not in the mood to play games with his wife. "Then why did you call and say it was urgent that I call you back? I tried to call your cell and the house but finally gave up and left a message. I know it wasn't anything to do with Madison, so are you playing games now?"

"Bernard, what are you talking about? I haven't called since you left. Actually, I've been with Ananda. We went shopping and then I had some meetings."

Concentrating on what she was saying, Bernard's mind began to race once again. Lisette didn't go out much but when she did it was usually with Ananda Cannady, her closest friend. And he had found it strange that she'd called the resort with her urgent message and not his cell phone. The fact that she'd been unavailable when he called back only made the situation seem a little more odd.

Then he'd remembered that as the hotel clerk had been knocking on his door, his own cell phone had also

been ringing. Walking to the dresser where he'd placed
his phone upon entering the room, he immediately
scrolled the missed calls. There was an unavailable number listed at yesterday afternoon at 2:35—the exact time
he was in the spa room with Casey.

"Bernard? Are you still there?" Lisette was saying.

He held in a curse and dropped his cell phone back on
the dresser. "Yeah, I'm here. Don't worry about it. The
clerk must have gotten the wrong message," Bernard
said but knew that was impossible. In addition to telling
him about the urgent call the clerk had also given
Bernard a handwritten message with his wife's name and
cell phone number on it. There was no way the man had
pulled that information out of thin air.

"What's going on with your father and this political
strategist guy?" he asked, changing the subject.

"Oh, he called you about that already? We just met with
him two nights ago. Anyway, he thinks you have a good
chance of taking Dale Leidenman's spot in the Eighth
District next term. Leidenman's about to be indicted on
those money-laundering charges that surfaced last year."

Wasn't that a trip? Bernard was going to slip into politics on the tailwind of another man's misfortune. But
then, that's how the game was played.

"Yeah, I kind of thought he'd catch the rap for that
whole organization." He was rubbing the bridge of his
nose now, trying to get a grip on all that was happening.
"So I'll be back sometime tomorrow night, supposedly to
meet with your father and Perry Sunder."

"That's great you're coming home early. Maybe you
could take Friday off and we can spend the day together."

She sounded hopeful and young and loving and
Bernard cringed. He didn't want to hear any of that, not
from her. "I don't know. I just had some issues with the
commercial so I'm going to be pretty busy tomorrow

making sure everything works out before I have to leave. I'll probably spend Friday troubleshooting from the office." Or wondering what was going on with Casey. Because she was still heavily on his mind. What had happened between them last night and her disappearance today just wasn't adding up.

Lisette cleared her throat. "Bernard, we need to spend some time together. We need to talk . . . about our future."

There was a slight desperation to her words but Bernard opted to ignore it. "Not now, Lisette. I've got a lot going on at the moment. It'll have to wait."

"I don't think it can," she said and took a deep breath. "There are some things we need to work through, some issues that need to be resolved."

"Didn't you hear me say I had other things going on? I don't have time for your drama right now."

"Oh really?" There was a hitch in her voice and then she said coolly, "Do you have time for the whore you're sleeping with? Who's the flavor for this month, Bernard? And when is she going to get the boot so you can move on to the next one?"

A chill ran down Bernard's spine at her words. So she knew. He'd wondered how long he'd be able to go on with the affairs without her ever saying a word. In fact, her silence all these years had been another issue in their relationship. What type of woman sat back and let her husband cheat on her? And was that the type of woman he wanted to be married to?

"Not now, Lisette," he said sternly.

"Then when? After you've finished with her? Or just before I file for divorce?"

She'd hung up the phone then and Bernard had cursed fluently before going to stand on the balcony. He inhaled deeply, taking in the scenery. The sun was just setting, tinting the sky in a deep gray, streaked with fierce orange and slashes of yellow. Palm trees blew in the breeze, their limbs like arms stretching across the horizon, reaching for something they might never find. No matter how much they swayed and reached, when the wind ceased they returned to their sedated stance, empty-handed.

That's exactly how Bernard felt, as if he'd been reaching for something for far too long to still be standing on this balcony, empty-handed.

"I'm beginning to think that maybe I shouldn't have given you a key," Nola said as she dropped her suitcase just inside her front door.

Gee was once again sitting in her living room, waiting for her.

"If we lived together giving me a key wouldn't be an issue," he replied, then stood and walked toward her.

"I don't know how many times I have to—"

Now standing directly in front of her, Gee put a finger to her lips, stalling her words. "Let's not argue. You've been gone too long."

Folding her into his arms, he kissed her long and slow, erasing the argument that had been on Nola's tongue, replacing it with those mingling doubts that assaulted her mind all throughout her plane ride. She didn't love Gee. She knew she didn't because she wasn't capable of loving anyone in that way. Deep down Nola knew the reason that she could never love was rooted in the fact that she'd never felt love. Her father had neither loved nor wanted her, while her mother did her best to make up for the man who had broken both their hearts.

The emptiness was still there. The bitterness continuously leaking into her system like a busted pipe.

Gee's hands moved up and down her back, caressing

her, not gently and not roughly. In a few minutes he'd be grabbing her ass, then he'd lift her, press her back to the wall and rub his erection against her jean-clad pussy. That's what she needed. Hot, rough sex. That's what she always needed. It was the only thing that softened the edge of pain that kept the worst of the memories and sorrow at bay.

But as he continued to kiss her, Nola was startled. That's all he did was kiss her. His lips moved over hers possessively as they normally did but yet they were laced with something else. He held her in his firm embrace. It felt like a shield, his arms around her, sheltering her. She pressed her breasts into his chest, opening her mouth wider, thrusting her tongue deeper to let him know she was ready for the next step.

Still he held and kissed her, only.

Nola's mind raced even as her body heated. She needed him inside her. She needed him on top and behind her. She simply needed him. That in and of itself was a change, because Nola never needed anybody. But right now, at this very moment, if she didn't have him, if they didn't have sex she would scream. She would yell. She would most likely lose her mind or worse, she might even cry—the emotions bubbling inside her were so intense.

When he still made no move to oblige her needs, Nola pulled away, squirming out of his reach.

"What the hell is wrong with you?" she screeched.

"There's nothing wrong with me, baby. I just missed you."

"Well then, why don't you act like it?"

For a moment Gee simply stared at her, puzzled. This was the woman that he loved. The woman he wanted to spend the rest of his life with, and yet there were times when he wasn't quite sure she even liked him. For instance, right now she was looking at him as if she could barely stand the sight of him.

Clenching his fists at his side and letting them go, Gee took a deep breath. "Do you want me to go?" he asked, praying that she would say no. Knowing that if she said yes, he would argue to stay.

"If you're gonna be here in my apartment waiting for me each and every time I return, I'd like a proper welcome home."

"And that would be different from what I just gave you, how?"

"You know what I'm talking about. You know what's between us. There's no sense in playing games or talking our way around it."

Gee nodded, slipping his hands into his pockets as he watched her move about the apartment. She went to the table, picking up a stack of mail, then flipping through it, dropping it and going to the minibar in the corner of her living room. She grabbed a glass to fix herself a drink. It was almost eight o'clock in the evening so she'd no doubt be ready for a glass of vodka.

Nola wasn't an alcoholic but when she needed a drink, she needed something strong.

"So every time you return you want me to be here naked, waiting to fuck you. Is that what you're saying?"

She poured the clear liquid into the glass, then caused a clanking sound as she slammed the bottle down. Casting him an irritated look, she lifted the glass to her lips and took a deep swallow.

"I don't expect anything from you, Gee," she said, setting the glass carefully on the bar after her drink. "All I'm saying is we have a system, you and I. It's just what we do. It's what we've done since the very beginning."

"Things have changed since the very beginning, Nola."

She was already shaking her head. "No. They haven't. We're still here to provide each other's pleasure."

"Are you sure? Is that all? I'm only good enough to fuck you but I shouldn't care about you. I shouldn't want more from you."

"No! You shouldn't!" she yelled, then slammed both her palms down on the bar and stared down at her glass. "You can't," she said in a voice much smaller than before.

"I don't want to fuck you all the time, Nola," he stated and took careful steps toward where she stood. Nola was a strong, independent woman. She didn't need anybody for anything. Gee knew this and still he wanted to be there because some part of him understood Nola's struggle. He knew what she wouldn't even admit to herself.

"That's not what I want. I don't want you to care for me and I don't want you to be with me. It's just sex. Sex is good. It's easy. Why can't we just keep it that way?"

Gee stopped short just a few feet from her. "Because I want more," he said seriously. "And because you deserve more."

She shot him a heated glare. "You don't know me. Don't presume to tell me what I need."

"I know you're hurting, that you've been hurt so badly that you're scarred from the inside out. I know that you don't believe you need any help and healing and I also know that if I don't stop you, you're damn sure gonna self-destruct.

"You're spiraling out of control, Nola. You think you're on the right track, doing what needs to be done for all the damaged and confused women of the world, but you're not, baby. You're just inching closer to falling off that cliff. And I'll be damned if I'll sit back and watch you do it!"

"Just go home!" Nola cried, running her fingers through

her short hair and moving from around the bar to push past him.

Gee gave her a few minutes, then followed her into the bedroom. She'd already removed her blouse and was unbuttoning her jeans when he stood in the open doorway.

Nola looked up when she heard him approach. "It's too late now, I don't even want to have sex with you," she said flippantly.

With a crooked smile, Gee made his way into the room, removing his own shirt as he came closer to her. Nola had just gotten her legs out of her jeans and was standing in front of her dresser when he approached. With a gentle hand he cupped her cheek and lifted her face to his.

"What? You didn't hear what I said?" Her tirade began again.

"Shhhh," he whispered and miraculously she acquiesced.

"I don't want to fuck you, Gee. Not anymore."

Before she could speak another word Gee touched his lips to hers, gently letting his tongue caress the lower one lovingly. Her palms instinctively lifted, pressing flat on his chest. His hands moved down her shoulders to her back and further still until he had lifted her into his arms, wrapping her legs securely around his waist. He turned and walked her to the bed where he lay her down gently.

Her mouth had said she didn't want to have sex with him but that had been a lie. He'd known it just as she had. His nimble fingers made quick work of getting her naked. She squirmed beneath him because he still wore his pants and shoes.

"Calm down, baby. Let me take care of this," he whispered, then pulled up from her and removed his final pieces.

Nola lay patiently, which was new for her, waiting for his return. Something in the air had changed but she didn't want to think too hard on it. She wanted just what she'd wanted when she first walked in, to lose herself in the delicious euphoria of great sex. There was the only place where she didn't have to think, didn't have to concentrate on the intricacies of life. She was free, once and for all.

Naked now, Gee climbed on top of her. Nola quickly spread her legs, lifting her hips to greet him. He knew what she was doing. Hiding. But he wasn't going to allow her to do it any longer.

"Look at me," he directed her.

She did and what he saw in her eyes was impatience, desire so thick he could slice it with a knife, and just a tinge of fear. His heart ached and he wanted desperately to take that away from her, to take all the worry and anger away from her. But Nola wasn't trying to hear any of that, at least not in the way he'd previously tried to reach her. He prayed that this way would prove more effective.

Lowering his head, he kissed her, keeping his eyes fastened on hers. While their tongues dueled their eyes locked, meeting in a furious struggle that threatened to make or break them.

Around his hips he felt her thighs relax slightly. A moan escaped her throat and she slowly lifted her arms to wrap around his neck. Yes, he thought, she was letting him in.

Because his dick was hard as steel and giving him a very painful indication that playtime was over, Gee rotated his hips, adjusting himself and aiming for her sweet center. When his tip touched her damp core her eyes rolled back, her back arched and she pulled her lips away from his to whisper his name.

He pushed forward, sliding deep inside her in one

swift motion. She bucked, trying to increase his depth.
Nola loved him to go deep, but Gee held back. In fact, he
pulled out of her only to hear her whimper in disap-
proval.

Slipping back inside was torture to his body but music
to his soul the moment her nails tapped into his skin, his
name a sweet melody on her lips. This would be different, just as he'd told her. He didn't—wouldn't—fuck her
anymore. He was in love with her and it was time she
knew it, got used to it, accepted it.

Nola lay beside Gee, her ass snuggled tight against his
now semi-erect dick. Even in sleep the man was aroused.
They were insatiable together and she'd liked that. No,
she'd *loved* that.

She'd wanted to get lost in the sex, in the blur of sensations so she didn't have to think of her pain or her fear.
Instead she'd gotten something else. She knew that had
been Gee's intention all along. He'd put his words into
motion. With each stroke of his dick he'd pumped his
feelings deep inside her until she felt full, overflowing
with foreign emotions that threatened to choke her.

Laying naked beneath him as he'd poured his essence
freely into her body, Nola felt exposed, more so than her
simple nudity provided. He'd looked down at her as his
face had contorted with deep-felt pleasure. His eyes had
held hers, conveying a message so loud her eardrums almost exploded. She'd tried to turn away, to look at the
wall, at the furniture, at anything but him. He'd grasped
her chin roughly, turning her back.

"Don't hide from me, Nola. Not now. Never again."

His words had been gruff, his chest still heaving as
he'd tried to steady his breathing.

She didn't speak, didn't want to say anything for fear
of what it might be. A thousand thoughts swirled through

her mind, some she was used to, others she couldn't stand. Instinct had her moving, trying to get away from him.

But he grabbed her, wrapping his thickly muscled arms around her and holding her tight. "I'm not letting you go. Ever. So get used to it."

After a few minutes she knew the struggle was futile so she stopped. He rolled to the side and surprised her by keeping her folded in his embrace.

She didn't like the confinement. She enjoyed the protection. She had to get up. Her body wouldn't move.

Fuck! Her mind screamed even as her heart slowed to a steady rhythm that matched his.

"He wants a commitment and you're running away."

"I'm not the one who runs away," Nola said, dropping down into the leather recliner in the basement of Steven's town house where Cally now lived. After Nola had been sure Gee was soundly asleep, confirmed by the drop of his bottom lip and the soft snore emanating from his throat, she'd driven over to Cally's in desperate need of advice.

"Girl, please, you're running so fast I can see the dust circles forming behind you."

"Not funny," Nola quipped, rolling her eyes.

"Not meant to be funny. It's meant to be real. You've been running from a relationship for a long time now, Nola. You had to know that you couldn't keep going through life fucking this man and that man and never slow down."

"And why can't I? If that's the way I want to live my life then who is he to come along and think he can change that?"

"Maybe he's the man who loves you."

"Bullshit! He doesn't love me. He may love this pussy,

but he doesn't love me. I'm not about to fall for that fluffy fairy-tale shit you and Serena are all hooked up in. You know that's not how I roll."

"Apparently, you're not sure how you roll or you wouldn't be sitting in my basement at three o'clock in the morning looking like a cross between a broken-hearted teenager and a pissed-off sista."

"I am pissed off."

"Why? Because he said he cared about you? Or because he said he didn't want to fuck you anymore?"

"Not that. That's just words."

"It's not just words and you know it. That's why you're pissed off. You know he's serious and you're scared."

"Cally, men don't scare me."

"Men may not scare you, but apparently Sgt. Gee does."

Nola huffed, rolled her eyes, then let her head fall back on the chair. "This is just not me. I can't do this."

"Why can't you do it? You sell yourself short all the time. You let that no-good asshole of a father destroy your life. The life that he didn't give a damn about being involved in. But yet you let him take control of you."

"He doesn't control me and he doesn't control my life." Nola listened to her words and realized that Cally might just be right. And hadn't her mother said essentially the same thing? For so long she'd thought she was the strong one. The one who put her father out of her mind since he clearly didn't want to be in her life. She'd thought she was over what he'd done to her and her mother. Maybe she'd been wrong and his actions had been controlling hers all this time.

"Stop the bullshit, Nola! He's been controlling you since the day he walked out. Everything you've done in your life has been either to prove that you were good enough or that you were better than the man that walked out on you. Your mother has spent all her years pining away, her heart still broken by him. So much so that she couldn't even start a new relationship with another man. Now, is that what you want for yourself?"

She sighed, not liking the direction of the conversation but realizing its importance. "Relationships aren't all they're cracked up to be, Cally."

"Do you really believe that or are you just trying to convince yourself? No, don't answer," Cally said, holding up her hands. "Let me tell you what I know about you, because despite what anybody else says I know you better than you know yourself. You want a relationship. You want what your mother never had. You want it so bad that it hurts. And that hurt fuels your anger. That anger can only be directed at the man who took this dream away from you. You walk around with this humongous chip on your shoulder, aiming it at every man who lives and breathes. And it's not fair. You've done this for years and finally a man has come along and knocked that chip right off your shoulder."

"Forever the writer," Nola said dismally. "You and your fancy dialogue. Look, you're right, you do know me and it's because of that I'm going to cut the bullshit and put all my cards on the table."

Nola sat up, propping her elbows on her knees. "I'm afraid, Cal."

Cally didn't speak, simply lifted a brow, waiting for her to continue.

"I'm afraid of exactly what you said, living my entire life without ever having a real relationship, just like my mother. The problem with that fear is, there's a lot of anger attached to it. A part of me doesn't want to take that chance. Hell, look what happened with Jenna and Mark or Drew or whatever the hell his name was. Look how that turned out!"

"Everybody's entitled to a mistake.

"I talked to Mama this morning and she said Jenna and her new husband had moved to the Islands."

"Phff, to the Islands? That is not going to help his balls grow back," Nola said flippantly.

Cally chuckled. "Now girl, you know that's not right. I still can't believe you shot him in the balls."

"Believe it. I did it and I'd do it again. See, that's what I'm saying. How could I be in a relationship? How can I fall in love with a man and still have that type of anger in me that I could shoot his balls off if he crosses me?"

"What you should be asking yourself is, how could a man who knows that you're capable of shooting his balls off the minute he pisses you off, fall in love with you? That's the million-dollar question."

Chapter 16

"Son of a bitch!" Bernard cursed when he'd opened the envelope, saw the picture, then watched as the lone ivory business card fell to his desktop.

The picture was of him and Casey in the Jacuzzi at the Horizon. The card read: *Breakdown, Inc.—When it's time for a woman to get even.*

He slammed his fist down on his desk and spun around in the chair until he could see the full view of Baltimore's Inner Harbor.

This was not happening. It could not be happening. And yet, with an intake of breath and a flaring of his nostrils, Bernard knew that it was.

He recalled the phone call he'd received prior to entering his office.

"Bernard Williamson?" the female voice had asked when he'd answered his cell phone as he climbed out of his car in the office parking lot.

It was Friday afternoon and he'd had a brunch meeting with Arnold, Perry, and the mayor at the yacht club. He still didn't want to deal with the confrontation he knew was coming with Lisette so he'd opted to go to the office for a couple of hours.

"Yes?"

"I've got a deal for you."

"Who the hell is this?" He frowned and stepped onto the elevator, pressing the button that would take him to the main level where he could board the elevators to the top floors.

"That's not important. What's important is your wife and the way you decide to handle this situation."

"What situation?" Gut instinct had Bernard's head throbbing instantly. He was not liking the direction of this conversation.

"She knows you're a lying, cheating bastard and she's sick and tired of it. So here's what you're going to do."

The list of things this woman said was almost laughable except Bernard sensed how serious she was.

"Who the fuck are you to call me saying some dumb shit like this? What goes on between me and my wife is our business. I'll have your ass locked the fuck up for calling me with this nonsense. And talking about my daughter and her trust fund, that's way out of order!"

He was yelling as he entered the second elevator and tried to contain his anger as he punched the button to his floor with fury.

"I'm the one woman that isn't afraid of nor turned on by you. And that makes me your worst enemy. You've got twenty-four hours to do what I've said or the shit will definitely hit the fan."

She hung up! He couldn't fucking believe she'd dropped her bombshell and hung up on him. No, what he couldn't believe was that he'd just been threatened by someone he didn't even know. But he'd bet a dollar to a dime that Lisette knew.

So as he marched down the halls of CCM toward his

office, he punched in her cell number. Surprise, surprise, the voice mail clicked on.

Bitch!

Bernard stormed into his office and slammed the door. Dropping his briefcase on the edge of his desk, he sank into his chair and was about to pick up the phone to call his house when he saw the envelope.

Now he sat staring out the window on a cloudy Saturday afternoon wondering what step he was going to take next.

If he were a violent man he'd go right home and choke the life out of Lisette for being stupid enough to hire that psychotic Nola Brentwood to do her dirty work.

Bernard had read in the papers and watched with amazed horror as the once powerful attorney had been on trial for shooting her cousin's fiancé in the balls. She'd served a meager sentence in jail, to his estimation, and was apparently now out on the loose again. Damn the justice system! And damn bitter, crazy-ass women!

Meosha put her key into the door with a heavy sigh. The Antigua trip hadn't turned out the way she'd expected. Still, it had its high points.

One of them was meeting Nola Brentwood. On the plane ride home she couldn't help but replay the time she and Nola had spent together, coupled with the night they'd spent with Bernard. Of course, Meosha knew that was the last time she'd ever sleep with Bernard so she'd been determined to make it the best.

And it was.

What she wrestled with was whether or not it was the best because of Bernard and his sexual prowess—even while intoxicated—or because of Nola's presence.

The evening had stretched into the early morning hours as she and Nola had pushed Bernard to the brink of coming then watched as he struggled with control. Nola had straddled his face, feeding him the pussy Meosha knew was sweet as honey, while she had sucked his dick with the urgency that she knew drove him crazy. He'd pumped into her mouth frantically while Nola had grasped the headboard and thrust her hips over his face.

Meosha could only imagine how the scene would play back on the DVD and couldn't wait for Nola to provide her with a copy.

It was with tired limbs, a slightly aroused body, and a leery sense of something amiss that Meosha entered the condo. In the distance she heard the shower running and figured Kalita was just getting home from work and settling in for the night.

Meosha swore, that girl rarely went out, except with that tired-ass man she was messing with. Kalita was an attractive girl, so Meosha couldn't understand why she continued to sell herself short. That's why Meosha refused to commit to any man. All they could do for her was sex her and pay her. There was no room in her life for anything else.

Women like Kalita gave her a headache. They were always waiting for that happy ending, that fairy-tale love-of-their-life bullshit that Meosha refused to subscribe to. And it wasn't because she'd had her heart broken before, because Meosha played her cards to ensure that she'd be the one doing the heart breaking, not the other way around. For her it was more of a survival instinct. Too many women depended on men for their means of survival and Meosha didn't want to go that route. She wanted to live her own life, on her own terms and she was doing just that.

Going into her room, she dropped her bags and thought she'd take a shower herself but knew she'd have to wait for Kalita to finish. For all the money they were paying for this condo the water pressure was the pits. So she slipped out of her shoes and lifted her hair off her neck, snagging a scrunchie off her dresser as she left her room again.

Securing her hair into a loose knot at the top of her head, she headed for Kalita's room. She'd poke her head into Kalita's bathroom, let her know she was home, then fix a quick snack while waiting for Kalita to finish in the shower. Thoughts of a ham and cheese sandwich and a nice, hot shower were on Meosha's mind as she walked into the other bedroom.

The next events would have made her puke had she actually eaten that sandwich first.

In the middle of Kalita's bed was a man, a dark-skinned man with a tight ass and muscled legs. He lay on his stomach, his boxer shorts stretched tightly over his ass due to the way his legs were spread. His chest was bare, his face turned to the side on one of the many pillows Kalita kept on her bed.

Something vaguely familiar stirred in the pit of Meosha's stomach and she took another step closer to the bed. A voyeur she definitely was not, but then again, this wouldn't classify as voyeurism since the man was clearly asleep. What she knew for a fact was that this was not the deadbeat that Kalita was messing with. She knew this because he was a high yellow brotha with that too pretty, too curly hair that convinced him that he was the shit, when he actually wasn't worth shit.

So what had Kalita been up to while she'd been gone? Meosha thought back to her assessment of her roommate and best friend just a few minutes ago, in which she'd been worrying about her friend's lack of dating experience, or lack of common sense, when it came to men, whichever. Apparently, she'd been way off the mark in her assessment because it looked like Kalita had been getting her freak on.

Meosha was just a few inches away from the side of the bed where she could get a better look at the man's face when the ball of her foot connected with something sharp on the floor. She yelped and immediately knelt to the floor to see what the damage was.

On the bed, the man jumped up, looking around the room to see from where the noise had come.

"Shit!" Meosha cursed, knowing she'd have to come up with a damn good reason why she was in Kalita's room gawking at her half-naked lover. Only when Meosha looked up and caught the gaze of said lover, her eyes locked with familiar ones and she gasped.

"Cam?"

He rubbed his eyes. "Meosha."

At that exact moment it dawned on Meosha that the water from the shower had stopped. Kalita now stood in the doorway of the bathroom. "Meosha? You're home early."

Rising slowly from the floor, Meosha looked from Cam—her ex-boyfriend, to Kalita—her soon-to-be ex-roommate. "What the hell is going on here?" she asked without preamble.

"It's not what you think," Cam was already saying as he scrambled up off the bed, wisely on the opposite side from where Meosha stood.

"Oh, it's not? You don't have a clue what I'm thinking," she yelled.

Kalita crossed her arms over her chest, wearing the thigh-length robe she'd donned when she stepped out of the shower. "I've known you for a long time so I can imagine what you're thinking. But like Cam said, it's not like that."

"It's not? So what you're telling me is that just because I walked into my roommate's room, found my man laying in her bed just about naked and her coming out of the shower just about naked, it doesn't mean that they've been fucking while I've been away."

Cam was the first to interrupt. "Your man? Oh, I'm back to being your man now? Funny, that's not what you were saying that day in court."

Then Kalita chimed in. "First of all, you shouldn't be jumping to conclusions. I can't believe you would even think that I would sleep with a man you used to be involved with. *Used to be*, being the operative phrase here."

Meosha waved her hand through the air, dismissing both of their comments. "None of that means a damned thing. The bottom line is you're fucking Cam! When I left here you had the audacity to scold me about dating a married man and then you turn around and sleep with my boyfriend."

Meosha headed across the room toward Kalita. Cam took a defensive step in front of her. He was a man and all but there wasn't about to be a chick fight in this room. Not over something as stupid as this misunderstanding. But what really bothered him was the way Meosha kept referring to him as her man.

For the months that he'd slept with her, the months that he'd fallen in love with her and wanted her to be so much more to him than just a sex partner, she'd been nonchalant. The last nail in his coffin, the knock on the head that his family said he'd needed, was the day she testified in court that the barbershops he'd owned were funded by drug money. That statement caused him to lose everything he'd worked so hard for and drew the attention of FBI agents as well as local law enforcement agencies. He'd come back only because he'd found evidence that maybe, just maybe, Meosha had been forced into her testimony. He'd wanted to hear her side, wanted with a part of him that worked on sheer desperation, to hear her say that she still loved him and had never meant to hurt him.

But standing here now, watching her reaction, all he could feel was confusion.

"Hold up. Hold up. Both of you just calm down. Like she said, Meosha, it's not like that."

"Then what is it like? What the hell are you doing here anyway? And what are you doing in here with her if it's not like that? Has this been going on for the last year behind my back?"

"Like I would be sleeping with him behind your back for a whole year. Come on now, Meosha, you know me better than that. Plus, I got a man," Kalita yelled.

"You got a sorry-ass man, so I guess you figured you'd latch on to one of mine."

"Girl, not hardly. What makes you think I'd want your leftovers? They aren't good for anything but lying and cheating on their wives."

Around him the bickering just kept going until Cam had heard enough. "Be quiet!" he yelled and received venomous glares from each of the women, just as he'd expected. Not so much that they were going to listen to what he'd said, but the fact that he'd yelled had taken their attention away from each other and put it back on the matter at hand.

"This is how it went down. I left New York a few days ago and came back here to see you. When I showed up, Kalita said you weren't here. She said I could crash here until you got back. Plain and simple."

"She said you could crash here or she said she would sleep with you? Which one was it?"

"I said, he could crash here! I didn't think you'd want your ex sleeping in your bed so I let him sleep in mine."

"And you're just coming out of the shower while he's laying in the bed half-naked, why?"

"As if I owe you any further explanation, because I came into my bathroom where all my personal items were to take the damn shower. But you know what, Meosha, I see now that clearly our friendship isn't as strong as I thought it was. If you could come in here and take the circumstances at face value and not even give me the benefit of the doubt, then to hell with you. You can keep right on thinking that I slept with *your man*. How does it feel to find out that somebody's cheated on you? The shoe's on the other foot now, huh. You're not the mistress, you're the victim!" With that Kalita stomped out of the room, leaving Cam and Meosha alone.

"We didn't sleep together," Cam said when Meosha's gaze once again fell to him.

"Whatever, Cam. I don't even care."

"Obviously you do. Which I find sort of unbelievable considering the way we parted."

"The way we parted? Your ass was hauled off to jail, that's the way we parted."

"Because of the lies you told on the stand."

"Lies? I know you're not coming up in here to accuse me of lying and that's why you got locked up."

"That's exactly what I'm telling you and I want to know who put you up to saying it. Who told you that my money came from selling drugs?"

"Nobody had to tell me anything. I'm not stupid."

"Clearly you are if you dismissed everything I told you. I told you where I got the money from."

"Yeah, yeah. Some lawsuit where you were in a car accident when you were young and had some injuries to your back."

"Some injuries to my back? I have permanent damage to two of the discs in my spine. You weren't even listening. You didn't even pay enough damned attention to me to hear when I was telling you something important about my past."

"I don't give a shit about your past, Cam! I didn't then and I damned sure don't know. Especially now that I see what type a man you really are."

"You don't have a clue, Meosha. Not one clue what type of man I am. But I'm starting to see, for once, the real woman that you are."

"That's right. I'm a real woman. One that you can't fool with this bullshit. I don't want to hear about that court date, my testimony, your barbershops, none of that nonsense. That's yesterday's news. When I walked out of that courtroom I walked out of your life."

"That's right," Cam roared. "You walked out of my life. You left me with absolutely nothing but the feds on my ass. My business was gone, the woman I thought I loved was gone. I had nothing. I had to go back to New York and start all over again."

With a nod of her head and a quirk of her lips Meosha quipped, "Exactly. You went back to New York and did what? How did you start over again, Cam? Did you sell some more drugs and make yourself some more money and come back here to open up yet another barbershop? Exactly what do you mean by 'start all over again'?" She didn't wait for a response but put her hand up in his face. "You know what, never mind. I don't even want to know. The point is you brought your trifling ass back in my house and fucked my best friend—or should I say my supposed best friend. Fuck you and her! I don't have to take this bullshit!"

With those last words Meosha turned and left, slamming the door to Kalita's bedroom.

Her heart pounded in her chest as she moved to her room and picked up the suitcases she'd sat there earlier.

She was on her way out the front door when she heard Kalita's voice.

"You know you're wrong," she said.

Meosha stopped, turned and looked at the one woman she thought was on her side in this crazy world. "No. What I know is you're a backstabbing slut and I'll never forgive you for this."

Chapter 17

Casey had been back from Antigua for a full day now, but Simon wasn't home. He'd left a note with his itinerary—he was in Miami on a photo shoot. He'd be back some time tonight.

For the last few days Casey had been trying to put some things into perspective—her life, her goals, her dreams, her wants, her desires. At one time she thought they all were connected. She thought she had everything sorted out. Now, after being in Bernard's arms, after coming so close to having sex with him, she was totally confused.

Then again, being with Bernard had cleared up at least one aspect of her life—she and Simon were through. No matter how much she'd fought it, she now knew what she had to do. She couldn't force Simon's hand. She'd never be able to live happily if she thought he was marrying her just because of the ultimatum she'd made. They'd had this conversation over and over again and Simon was right, it was like beating a dead horse. He wasn't going to change his mind and she wasn't going to change hers. Their outcome had been staring her in the face for months, she'd just refused to accept it.

Until now.

She'd had the time to completely think things through and knew what her next move needed to be. She would leave Simon. She had enough money saved up so that she could get a place of her own, but that would take a few weeks at least. Could she stay here with Simon for another few weeks knowing that their relationship was over and would he even want her to? One thing Casey knew for sure was that Simon wasn't going to take their breaking up lightly. He just wasn't that type of man. Not that he would get violent or anything, but they'd been through a lot together and she really didn't doubt his feelings for her, they just weren't enough.

So Casey had already begun packing. Actually, she'd started cleaning out her closet and putting things in boxes that she'd purchased from the office supply store on her way home from the airport. Her decision was made, it was just a matter of implementing the plan.

Funny thing was she didn't feel as sorrowful as she'd imagined she would. She was about to walk away from five years of her life and she really didn't feel anything—not sad and not glad. What did that say about the relationship between her and Simon?

Someone on the outside looking in would probably conclude that the decision to leave Simon was fueled by the time she spent with Bernard and they'd be partially right. Casey had deduced that if it was so easy for her to slip into Bernard's arms, to straddle him, eager to have sex with him, then what she felt for Simon must not have been strong enough. To marry Simon, she should love him, and only him with all her heart. Yet, she'd felt something for Bernard. No, it wasn't love; she wasn't naive enough to believe that's what the emotion was. But it was something, something she'd been willing to act on. That meant what she had with Simon wasn't what she thought it was.

She'd been trying not to think of Bernard and for the most part it was working. There was no future there, she knew that going in, something she'd wished she'd known with Simon. So since there was no future, Casey didn't really want to put too much time or energy into that situation. Facing him again on Monday morning at work would be soon enough for her to deal with what had happened in Antigua. But she'd deal with it in a professional manner. It would be Bernard's loss if he chose to handle things differently.

Casey knew that going to a different room and basically ducking out on him had been immature, but she'd needed time to get her thoughts in order, to think without him touching her, seducing her. And so she'd moved to the strictly au naturel building of the Horizon, barricading herself in her room so that she wouldn't be forced to walk around naked.

She'd continued to work on the commercial via phone calls to the producer and meeting with them privately. She didn't visit the set because she'd known that Bernard would be there. The producer didn't seem to mind either way as he wanted her and the rest of the CCM staff out of his hair so that he could do his job. So she'd been able to wrap up the commercial and actually couldn't wait to see the final production.

Casey continued to pack when her phone vibrated on her dresser. She'd turned the ringer off because she'd been receiving a bunch of hang-up calls from an unavailable number at all hours of the night. However, she hadn't wanted to totally turn her phone off for fear of missing an important work-related call or message. The incessant chiming was just getting on her nerves.

So she went to her dresser and looked down at the lighted window. It was a local number but it wasn't familiar. The mere fact that it didn't say *unavailable* meant that Casey was probably safe in answering it.

"Casey McKnight," she answered.

"Hey. Long time no see," he said.

Casey's heart thumped in her chest at the sound of Bernard's voice. "Hey," she finally managed. "How are you?" she asked, rubbing an already damp palm down her jean-clad thigh.

He hadn't called her in the days since they were together in the spa. Not one time had he called her cell phone to ask her what was going on. She wondered why he was calling now.

"I need to see you," he said simply.

She closed her eyes and took a deep breath. "No."

"Casey, please," he continued.

She was shaking her head although she knew he couldn't see her. "Bernard, I can't. Really, I'm busy right now."

"I wouldn't have called if it wasn't an emergency."

"Is it about the commercial?"

"No."

"Then is it about what happened between us on the island?"

"No." He sighed. "Well, sort of. Not really. Just . . . listen, I really need to talk to somebody right now. And the only person I can turn to is you. Could you meet me somewhere?"

She shouldn't. She knew she shouldn't.

She should hang up this phone and tell him she'd see him on Monday and that they could only discuss work issues. This was the right thing to do. Casey knew right from wrong, she'd always known. Her parents had beat it into her head so intensely, how could she ever forget? And yet, when her mouth opened the wrong thing inevitably came out: "Where do you want me to meet you?"

Casey parked her car in the garage of the Zenith, one of the newest luxury apartment buildings in downtown Baltimore. This was the address Bernard had given her, so she left the parking garage and took the elevator to the main floor where the doorman escorted her to the elevator that led to the residences.

The tall glass building was beautiful and boasted 360 degree views of the Inner Harbor and Baltimore's downtown district. Their office was only a few blocks from here in the World Trade Building, so Casey was very familiar with the area.

Bernard was at the door, opening it for her before she had a chance to knock. He looked as good as ever in his jeans and button-down white shirt. She didn't get a chance to see him in casual clothes often but readily admitted that he wore them as well as he did designer suits.

"Thanks for coming," he said, letting her in and closing the door behind him.

"It sounded serious," she said, clutching her purse on her shoulder, hoping her nervousness didn't show. "Is this your apartment?" she asked.

She was looking around now at the blond hardwood floors and vaulted ceilings. The living room was large and opened into the dining area. He had the horizontal blinds slightly opened so the cloudy sky peeked inside.

"Yeah," he answered.

"You stay here now that you're separated from your wife?" She continued moving further into the living room, dropping her purse on the very contemporary black couch.

For a moment Bernard was silent, then he answered, "Yes."

Casey nodded, then turned back to face him. "So what's going on? Why did you need to see me?"

She noted he looked tired and resisted the urge to go to him, to offer her support. Her presence would have to suffice.

"I don't know what's going on, Casey. I need to ask you a question and I didn't want to ask you over the phone."

"Okay," she said, noting the seriousness of his tone.

"Have a seat," he said and moved over the champagne-colored rug to take a seat in the matching chair sitting on the opposite side of a cream-checked coffee table.

Casey sat and crossed her legs. Bernard looked as if he were searching for the right words so she remained quiet, letting him get himself together. This place was lavishly furnished and looked as if he'd lived here for quite some time. She hadn't heard about his separation from his wife but it appeared he'd been telling her the truth. She wondered how she felt about that.

"Did you come to my room that night at the Horizon? Remember, we were supposed to meet."

She hadn't really expected this to be his question. She'd thought he'd want to talk about why she'd run away from him, but since she'd resigned herself to being totally honest with him she didn't let this question rattle her either way.

"No. I didn't," she answered.

Bernard closed his eyes and swore.

"Look, Bernard, I know you said you're separated and I know the way I acted in the spa may have given you the impression that I was game for this affair. But to be totally honest, I have a lot going on in my life. I've decided to leave Simon and I just don't know about being with you while you're still married."

She stopped, took a deep breath, and was about to continue when she noted his eyes were still closed.

"Bernard, are you okay?" she asked.

"No," he answered simply. Then he opened his eyes and focused on her. "But I will be."

"I don't understand. Is there something else going on?"

"Yeah. Somebody's into playing games." He stood and went to the window, his back facing her. "What they don't know is I don't lose. Ever."

Casey didn't know how to take his words. She didn't know what was going on but was almost positive that it didn't concern her. So she stood, grabbing her purse and prepared to leave. As she'd told him, she had enough going on in her life. "Look, this was a mistake. I'm going to just leave."

"No," he said quickly, turning to face her. "Don't go."

For endless moments they simply stood staring at each other. Then Bernard moved, coming to stand in front of her. Lifting one hand, he cupped her cheek. "I need you, Casey. Now, more than ever I need you."

Chapter 18

For the next forty minutes Bernard had kissed and licked every inch of Casey's body, until she lay limp in the center of his bed after multiple orgasms. The blinds in the bedroom were completely open so when he glanced toward them he saw Camden Yards amidst heavy dark clouds and a light sprinkling of rain. The perfect lovemaking weather.

He'd turned her on her stomach and now looked down at her beautifully plump ass. Her legs were opened a bit, he knew, because she was still adjusting herself to the anal plug he'd inserted inside her. Palming both her cheeks, he spread her open more to see her glistening with arousal.

She moaned as he lifted her hips up off the bed and his mouth watered. She was so open to him, so ready to do whatever he wanted. It had been hell all this time keeping his hands off of her and now that he had her he couldn't touch her enough.

"Bernard," she whispered. "I—" Her words ended as he touched his hand to the plug and slipped it free.

"Shhh, baby. I've got you."

And he did have her, just where he'd always wanted her. Rubbing a finger down the slit of her ass, he promised himself that after today no other man would have her again. His fingers slipped further between her legs, feeling the remnants of her orgasm and her arousal coating them. With slow, sensuous movements he brought his finger back to her ass, touching the sphincter now spread wider for him.

He slipped a finger inside and heard her moan louder.

"That's it, baby, you know I like to hear your pleasure. Louder," he said as he twisted his finger deep inside her rear.

She sucked in a breath and groaned, this time pushing back as he pushed in.

"That's it, baby. Take me deeper." Bernard released a groan himself and bit his bottom lip for control. "The way you're stretching around my finger. Damn. I'm trying to take it slow but I want you so badly."

"Please, Bernard. Please."

"Please what?" he asked, pulling out one finger then slowly trying two. With his other hand he held one cheek apart from the other so he could see his fingers sliding deep into her tight entrance. She was getting looser, her muscles flexing and opening for him. His dick thrust upward, dripping with incessant desire.

"Please . . . take . . . me."

She didn't have to say another word, those three were the sweetest he'd ever heard. Leaning over, he retrieved the tube of lube and one of the condoms he'd previously pulled from his nightstand drawer when they'd first entered the room. After sheathing his thick length, he squeezed a healthy portion onto his fingers that he rubbed up and down her ass, in and out of her rear until she was panting beneath him.

"Hold on, baby. Just a few minutes, I want to make sure you're ready."

This was her first time, Bernard knew. That, he readily admitted, was the fact that had his heart racing so fast. To know that he would be the first man to ever have her this way would earn him a definite place in her heart. Was that what he wanted?

Bernard couldn't think rationally at the moment. All he knew for sure was that if he didn't soon get inside her he would die. So filling his hand with lube again, he rubbed along the length of his dick, coating himself so that his entrance would be as painless to her as possible. He only wanted her to feel pleasure, complete unabated pleasure.

Bringing her up to her knees, Bernard leaned forward and kissed the small of her back. "Just relax, baby. I'm going to take good care of you."

She nodded, unable to speak and he rose over her, placing the thick head of his dick at her rear entrance. She shied away at the first touch and he rubbed her back.

"Casey, all you have to do is tell me to stop and I will." He didn't know where he'd gather the strength but he would definitely stop.

She relaxed. "I'm okay," she said, then let her hips fall loose into his hand, her legs spreading wider.

Again his tip touched her hole and he pushed forward. Casey's fingers tightened around the sheets as the first burning sensations rippled through her. This wasn't like his fingers or the plug he'd inserted earlier. This was bigger, it was harder, more persistent. And she wanted it. Oh, how she wanted it.

The mere thought of him entering her this way had been a source of erotic dreams since the first night he'd touched her there. She'd wanted to know how he would feel deep inside her rear, wanted to know how she would feel so fully stuffed with him.

This would be theirs alone, she thought. She'd never done this with any other man so once she'd been with Bernard this way, he would own her here. There was no question in Casey's mind. From this point on there was no going back. Not to Simon, not to her previous life, or her previous job. Things would be forever changed between them.

Unquestioningly she welcomed that change, pressing her ass back onto his dick with a motion so quick he gasped. The forced entry stung even more as her muscles stretched quickly. Biting down on her lip, she ignored the pain, knowing that pleasure was just a moment away.

He grabbed her hips and rotated his own. She felt him sinking further inside. She was tight back there, as an anal virgin ought to be. Still his thickness invaded, opening her, pleasing her.

Soon the worst was over and Casey was moving over his length with precision. Bernard's thrusts grew faster and Casey's breasts jiggled in response. He was riding the hell out of her and she felt like she was going to explode.

Reaching a hand around to touch her clit because it throbbed and begged for relief, Casey fingered herself. This too was new and intense. Her finger slid into her pussy without preamble as her thumb rested solidly on her clit. Bernard thrust deeper and deeper into her rear.

In her ears she heard her own voice yelling his name. Then she felt his fingers grabbing her wrist tightly, pulling her hand away from her pussy.

"I'm going to make you come. Just me, Casey. Just me," he groaned, then thrust his fingers into her pussy with more force than she had with her own.

He was fucking her fiercely then with his fingers and

with his dick. Casey was screaming by that point, her vision blurred, her mind locked solely on the pleasure he was providing.

Bernard was completely lost in her. Even as her body tensed and she came all over his hand he couldn't really focus. All he knew was the tightness of her muscles around his dick, the heady smell of their mixed arousals and the piercing sound of her screams.

It was blissfully erotic to be fucking her in the ass and pumping her pussy until she came. Her voice filtered through his mind, slipping down his spine with the smoothness of a shot of Hennessy.

His own guttural moan escaped as his balls tightened, his cum shooting in thick spurts into her canal.

He'd endured one of the most troubling mornings of his life only to have his afternoon completely erase that drama with the intenseness of their union.

Yes, Casey McKnight was meant for him, just as he'd thought the day he met her. Now he'd claimed her.

Leaning forward, he let her sated body fall. His dick was still seated tightly in her rear as he kissed her shoulder, then bit the damp spot, marking her, making her his, completely.

Cam couldn't believe his eyes.

He'd been following his buddy Gee's girl, just like he'd asked him to do. Cam needed the money and Gee had always been an excellent employer. So he'd taken the job, although he'd told Gee that any pussy that needed to be tracked wasn't worth the time it took to fuck her.

Gee's lady was everything Cam had expected and then some. She was fine, she lived in a tight-ass condo, drove a slick ole Mercedes, and walked with the class of the rich and famous. Too bad she was just as crazy and criminal as he was.

He'd followed her to her office building, which he thought was strange because it was Saturday afternoon. But then, Nola Brentwood didn't have a life unless it was ruining somebody else's. So he'd been tailing her and he was sitting outside the small building she rented in the Mt. Vernon district of Baltimore when he saw a car pull up and park in front of the building.

It was just an Acura, nothing too fancy and the rear tire was missing one of the Lorenzo rims. Cam was tapping his finger to the beat of Lil' Wayne's latest remix when all the breath was taken from his lungs.

Out of the Acura stepped Meosha.

He hadn't seen her since the day before at Kalita's place where she'd acted like the ass he now knew she was. She'd stormed out of the condo as if he'd been chasing her to give her ass the beatdown she deserved. Cam had never hit a woman but that day Meosha had come dangerously close to getting the taste slapped out of her mouth.

She'd lied on the witness stand and from the way she was talking she probably didn't have to be coerced to do so. She'd never loved him. And he should have listened to his family, who'd repeatedly tried to tell him that.

After she'd left, Cam had showered and sat in the living room talking to Kalita.

"Meosha's always been concerned with one person and one person only," Kalita had said as she opened another container of ice cream. That girl loved her ice cream. It was a wonder she wasn't bigger. He smiled at the memory.

Kalita was cool. She'd let him continue to crash at her place, giving him Meosha's room and her share of the bills at the same time. That was fine, he'd make the money to keep up his share of the bills and while he was at it he'd do something nice for Kalita. From what she'd told him last night when they'd sat in the living room watching another one of her chick flicks, her ex was the pits and she was coasting the single life just like him.

Yeah, he'd definitely do something nice for Kalita. Maybe buy her an outfit or something. She deserved somebody to be nice to her and Cam appreciated her company. Without her being there he didn't know that he would have been able to let Meosha walk out that door without hurting her. But Kalita had been the voice of reason.

"My mama used to tell me that you can't help a person that doesn't want to be helped. Meosha is fine with the way she lives her life. I'm through trying to stand in her way."

"I guess I should have listened to my family," he'd said dismally.

"I remember Meosha saying they didn't like her much,"

"Nah, they thought she was a gold digger."

Kalita chuckled. "You're right, you should have listened to them."

They'd both enjoyed the laugh and relaxed some more. It had been late when the movie ended and he'd stood to go to bed.

"Thanks for letting me stay here, Kalita," he'd felt compelled to say.

"Don't mention it. I can't afford this place by myself anyway."

He nodded. It was a nice condo so he figured it had to be pretty pricey. "It's cool. I'll do my part. You don't have to worry about that."

"I'm not."

"And," he said before moving to the bedroom. "You don't have to worry about all that bullshit Meosha was spouting. I'm not a drug dealer."

Kalita had cocked her head to stare at him, her dark curls framing her cinnamon brown face. "I believe you."

Never before had three words meant so much to Cam. So he was definitely going to do something more than nice for Kalita.

But right now, he was busy watching Meosha sashay her plump ass into the door of Breakdown, Inc. How did she know Nola Brentwood, he wondered. Then he thought, it didn't really matter. He was only hired to follow Nola and make sure no other man was hitting that.

Still, curiosity had him getting out of his car and walking across the street. As he approached the front window of Breakdown he saw Nola coming out of her office to greet Meosha. What he saw next caused a double reaction.

Meosha walked right up to Nola, opened her arms and hugged her. Nola hugged her in return then pulled back slightly to look at her. Then Meosha leaned forward, touching her lips to Nola's. The next thing Cam saw was the brief flash of tongues before they collided, Meosha's hands moving up and down Nola's back, then down to caress her ass.

His dick hardened at the same time his temples throbbed.

Cam whipped his cell phone out of his pocket and quickly dialed Gee's number. His man definitely wasn't going to believe this shit!

Chapter 19

The only words Gee heard were "Nola's with somebody." He'd been at work pulling a double when Cam had called him on his cell. He'd immediately stormed into his supervisor's office, telling him he had an emergency to take care of. His supervisor of six years wisely kept his mouth shut and nodded his understanding.

Gee had transferred from the Baltimore City Jail to Central Booking so it took him less than fifteen minutes to pull up in front of Nola's office. Once there, he jumped out of his truck and headed across the street toward the building.

Cam was standing out front smoking a cigarette, looking like an expecting father pacing back and forth. Gee only nodded toward him and reached for the handle to open the door. Cam grabbed his arm.

"Hold up, let me tell you what's going on first."

Gee pulled his arm away. "You told me enough."

"Nah, man, I don't think I did. See, I only told you that she was with somebody. I didn't tell you who the somebody was."

"Doesn't matter," Gee said, then pulled the door and stepped inside.

Cam cursed and followed behind him. He knew Gee was carrying at least two pieces. Cam had one himself nudging into his back beneath his long black T-shirt. As he'd been raised, Cam didn't believe in hurting women, but Gee didn't know that Nola was with a woman and Cam had no idea what Gee had been taught or what lengths he would take in the name of pussy.

So Cam stayed hot on his heels as he moved toward the back of the building where the offices were located.

Gee knew exactly where Nola's office was and stopped for one split second at the closed door. "I don't have to tell you that this stays between us, do I?" he asked without turning to Cam.

Cam inhaled deeply. "I got your back."

Gee nodded his bald head, then reached for the knob.

When they stepped inside, Nola was sitting in a chair facing the plasma television mounted on the far left wall. Meosha sat on the floor right beside her, one hand on Nola's while the other inched its way up between her legs.

Both women jumped at the intrusion. Meosha scrambled to close the buttons on her blouse but Nola, as Cam had previously conceded, was cool as a fan.

She spun around in the leather chair and looked at Gee with an amused expression. "Ever heard of knocking before you enter?" she asked calmly.

"You of all people should know that now is not the time to play dumb," Gee said, moving closer.

Meosha was up off the floor and had just glanced over Gee's shoulder to see Cam standing there.

"What the fuck are you doing here? Are you following me?"

Gee never looked away from Nola. "Take her to the truck," he instructed Cam.

Cam moved toward Meosha, who was cursing him like he'd already beat her. When he was close enough she swung on him, the palm of her hand landing against his cheek with a loud *crack*.

Cam cursed and again resisted smacking the hell out of her. Instead, he grabbed her still-swinging hands and turned her so that her back now faced his front. "Hit me again and you'll regret it," he whispered in her ear.

"Get your hands off me! I'll have your ass locked up again!" she was yelling when he lifted her off the floor and moved toward the door.

Once they were outside Nola's office he dropped her to the floor and watched with amusement as she crawled around trying to get away from him. Bending forward, he grabbed the back of her shirt and lifted her into the air once more. This time he backed her to the wall, slamming her against the drywall with considerable force.

"If you know what's good for you, you'll shut up all that damned noise. It's just going to piss me off."

"You are so out of your fucking mind! Why can't you get it through your head that I don't want you? I never did. Your were small-time. That's why I took the fifty thousand from Kane to set your dumb ass up. I hate you! I hate you!" she screamed.

All Cam heard was that she'd taken money to set him up. Kane had been his rival since high school over some petty shit that Cam could barely remember. But while he'd grown up and tried to live his life in peace, Kane had nursed his grudge, promising to pay Cam back. Well, he'd done that in spades, and Meosha had been the key.

Now, all bets were off.

Before he knew it his hands were around her neck

squeezing and squeezing until her ignorant words finally stopped. She was clawing at his hands, her eyes bulging in her head. Cam saw red, fury and hatred mixed with the feelings he thought he had for her.

Then, as if a bell went off in his mind, he let her go. She slid down to the floor, gasping and rubbing her neck. Moving to the front desk, Cam pulled open one of the drawers and found some huge rubber bands. He wrapped a few of them around his hand, then moved close to her again.

"Bastard!" she croaked as he grabbed her hands, pulling them roughly behind her back and wrapping the rubber bands around them tightly.

She was calling him a string of other names and Cam returned to the desk, found some scissors and cut a strip from his shirt. Balling it up, he waited until Meosha opened her mouth to call him another name and jammed it inside.

"Shut the fuck up!" he spat, then jerked her up again. This time he dragged her to the front door, out to Gee's truck and lifted the hatch to toss her into the cargo area beside the spare tire.

She looked up at him with pure hatred in her eyes and Cam smiled. "So you like to set people up, huh? Wait until you see what I've got in store for your trifling ass," he told her then slammed the door closed. Cam looked around quickly, hoping nobody had seen him. There was a baseball game today so most people in the downtown area were over near Camden Yards, not in Mt. Vernon. The streets were just about clear except for one or two cars going by occasionally. For now Meosha would have to sit tight. Cam wasn't sure where Gee's head was right now, so he needed to get back inside in case things got out of hand.

Moving back toward the building, Cam pulled out his cell phone.

"Yeah," he said when the person on the other end picked up. "It was Kane just like I thought. Handle it before I get back uptown."

"What am I going to do with you, Nola?" Gee asked, rubbing his hand down his face.

She was wearing a short dress that hugged her breasts, then flared at the waist, stopping barely mid-thigh.

"Nothing," she snapped. "I'm not your responsibility."

"No. You're my woman."

"No!" she screamed. "I'm not. But you refuse to understand that."

She'd stood from the chair and tried to walk past him. Gee grabbed her by the arm, spinning her around so that she was facing him again. "I love you, dammit!"

She glared at him. "I'm no romantic, but I'm almost positive that's not how you're supposed to declare your feelings for me."

"I'm not playing, Nola. I'm in love with you."

"Then you should accept me as I am," she said simply.

"As you are? What's that, Nola? Are you a lesbian, because I sure can't tell the way you crave my dick."

Nola shook her head, her eyes falling from his face. "No, Gee. I'm not a lesbian." But right at this very moment Nola wasn't sure what or who she really was.

"Then what the fuck were you doing with that woman? Why were her hands between your legs? Tell me what's going on here, Nola, so I can understand."

She pulled away from his grasp and was relieved when he didn't pull her back. Gee was seething mad and Nola was no fool. If he wanted to he could break her in two without a second thought. Yet she knew instinctively that he wouldn't.

Because he cared about her.

Since that night at her apartment, the night he'd made love to her instead of fucking her, she'd known that without a doubt. And after talking with Cally she'd finally admitted that she had feelings for him too. But where did that leave them? She still had a job to do, still had a commitment to her clients, a life she'd already begun to lead. How did Gee and his thoughts of a committed relationship fit into that scenario?

"She's nothing. Just somebody who helped me with a case," Nola admitted.

"And you paid her with sex?"

Nola spun around to face him. "No!"

"Then why was she touching you?"

She took a deep breath and figured if he said he'd loved her, just as she'd told him, then he needed to accept her for what she was. "We had sex but it wasn't for payment. That's not how I usually work my cases." She sighed wearily. "I was attracted to her so I did it. Case closed."

Gee swore. "You cheated on me with a woman?" he asked incredulously.

The way he said it made her sound smaller than the despicable men she dedicated her time to exposing. "I didn't cheat on you because we weren't together then," she snapped.

His stance relaxed a bit. "And are we together now?"

Nola leaned against her desk, her hands gripping the sides tightly. "I don't know. Are we?"

"Baby, I'm confused. You've got to just tell me what you want." His forehead creased as he raised his thick brows in question.

"What if I want you and her?" Which she didn't, because Meosha was clingy, unrealistic, and conniving. What

Gee had just walked in on was Nola showing Meosha the video that would break down Bernard Williamson. What Meosha was doing was trying to convince Nola to let her move in with her. To which Nola had already told her no. The plan was for her to show Meosha the tape, give her a copy, then send her on her way. There was nothing there between them. The night at the hotel had been good, for that night. But it wasn't something Nola wanted to continue.

Gee folded his arms over his expansive chest, his muscled legs spread in a defensive stance. His bald head glistened slightly and her fingers tingled with wanting to touch it. "Is that what you want? A threesome?"

Nola shrugged. "What if I did? Sometimes."

"Another woman?"

"Or another man?" she chanced.

"Hell no!" His response was immediate, his nostrils flaring, and Nola couldn't help but smile.

"I'm not playing, Nola. And I'm not sharing you with some other dude, so you can get that sick-ass thought right out of your mind. Hell, I don't want to share you with a chick either."

Nola could only shake her head. Gee didn't want to share her. He said he loved her. She wondered if she could take a chance at believing him.

Then he must have realized the DVD was still playing because he turned to the television screen.

Nola held her breath and waited for his reaction. He walked closer and watched as she and Meosha brought Bernard to climax.

He watched until the screen finally went black. Then he asked, without facing her. "Is that what your clients pay you for?"

She was a bit startled because she'd worn a wig when

she was with Bernard and Meosha. She hadn't wanted her identity revealed so she'd stayed out of the camera's view as much as possible.

"No, like I said before, I don't usually sleep with the clients or anyone else involved with a case. My clients pay me to get the goods on their husband. I figured there were really no rules to how I did that."

"Maybe you should reconfigure how you work your cases. Because this," he nodded toward the screen, "is taking it a little too far."

"I didn't think anybody would recognize me, that's why I—" she began, then sighed. He was right, she had gone too far with this one and now wondered how she was going to fix it.

He was turning to her, then shaking his head. "Don't even try it. I know every inch of your body. I don't care that you wore some cheap-ass blond wig or that your face was obscured." He was moving closer to her now.

"I know the curve of your ass, the tint of your nipples," he said and wrapped one arm around her waist. "You fucked him on tape!"

Nola's heart slammed against her chest. What was he going to do to her now that he knew?

"No. I didn't. You saw it for yourself. She fucked him, I only—"

"Say it, Nola! You only fed him your pussy, your tits! You kept him aroused while she fucked him!"

"I did my job!"

Gee pushed against her until she was bowed over the desk. With his other hand he pushed her skirt up around her waist. His fingers were rough as they pushed her thong aside then thrust viciously into her pussy.

She screamed, not in pain but in ecstasy. Her entire body trembled as she came instantly in his hand.

"Mine," he roared, then undid his pants and thrust his

aching cock inside her. "Fuck this job! You belong to me." His words were punctuated by his thrusts.

Nola's head fell back, her legs lifting to wrap around his waist.

"Yes!" she whimpered. "Yes!"

"Never again, Nola. Promise me that you will never do this again!"

Her arms clasped around his neck as Nola fought the raging storm within her. If she promised him she'd be trapped. She'd be his.

If she didn't he'd leave. Just like her father had.

When her legs trembled and his lips sucked at her neck, Nola gave up. She bucked one more time, felt her release washing swiftly through her body and whispered, "I promise."

Chapter 20

"Your plan didn't work," Lisette said when she'd stormed into Nola's office first thing Monday morning. "Bernard moved out of the house this weekend."

Nola was sitting behind her desk, typing a proposal for a new client whose husband was a reputed drug kingpin. She'd thought long and hard about taking this case because of the obvious implications of danger. But the woman was desperate and despite Nola's new outlook on things with her and Gee, she still knew all too well how it felt to be betrayed.

Turning her attention away from the computer to Lisette, Nola sighed. "Good morning, Lisette."

"Don't 'good morning' me. I paid you good money to make sure he did what I wanted him to do. And now he's gone. If I'd wanted him to simply leave I could have done that myself."

"Then why didn't you?" Nola asked.

"Because that's not what I wanted."

"You don't know what you want," Nola said, leaning forward and clasping her hands together on top of her desk. "You came to me saying you wanted to make him pay for his indiscretions and yet your price tag was a joke. I upped the stakes and he didn't bite. I told you that was a possibility."

"So what am I supposed to do now?"

"We blow his ass out of the water. That's what this was all about, Lisette. You see, there are two types of cheaters: ones with big brass balls and ones with no fizz to last more than three minutes. Bernard is shaping up to have pretty sizable ones, I must say."

Nola had known he wouldn't take the threat the moment she'd hung up the phone with him on Friday afternoon. Bernard Williamson was not a man to let go without a fight. So she'd known she'd have to show the DVD, that's why she hadn't minded giving Meosha a copy. Meosha would foolishly try to blackmail Bernard herself, to which she would get a rude awakening. The woman was no match for him.

Nola, on the other hand, knew just where to hit Bernard and how hard to punch.

"Don't worry about it. I have a meeting scheduled for tomorrow morning. After that, Bernard will have no choice but to come around."

Lisette still looked skeptical. "What meeting? With whom?"

"With Bernard, of course."

"Are you going to show him the DVD?"

"Yes."

"Has anyone else seen it?"

"No," she lied.

"Can I have a copy?"

Nola reached into her desk drawer and pulled out the

thin black case labeled *Williamson*. She reached over the desk, handing it to Lisette. "I have the master in a safe-deposit box. I'll take a copy with me to leave with Bernard tomorrow."

"What happens after that?"

"If all goes as planned his name will be off the accounts by the end of the week. Your lump sum will be in your account by month's end and divorce proceedings will be started. My job will be done."

"And my marriage will be over," Lisette said quietly.

Nola shook her head in pity. "Your marriage was over before it even began, Lisette. Everybody has known that but you."

"You're right, I've been a fool," Lisette said with a haunted look in her eyes.

For a minute Nola felt weird about the entire exchange. Then she chalked it up to Lisette's habit of flip-flopping moods. Nola would bet that Lisette Williamson was either bipolar or on the brink of losing her mind. But mental health was not her area of expertise. To that effect, Nola just wanted this case over with once and for all. "It happens to the best of us," she said, hoping she sounded compassionate enough.

"Thank you," Lisette said, standing from her seat. She looked down at herself, at the DVD she now held in one hand and gave a slight nod. Then her gaze returned to Nola and she attempted a slight smile before reaching across the desk to shake Nola's hand. "I appreciate all that you've done."

Nola stood, taking Lisette's hand and feeling a slither of dread through the connection. "It was my pleasure. I wish you and Madison the best of luck in the future."

Lisette nodded, turned and slowly walked away. Nola watched as she left her office, wondering what tomorrow's outcome would really bring. She knew that Bernard had a lot to lose at the airing of the tape. What she didn't know was whether or not he really cared. Another fleeting though had her turning her focus to Lisette and how the airing of the DVD would ultimately effect her.

Sitting back down, Nola put her head in her hands, wondering just when she'd changed from the vindictive private investigator to the sympathetic female, worried about the future of another one in her race.

Casey had moved out of the apartment she'd shared with Simon on Friday night, before he came home. After spending the afternoon with Bernard she'd had no other choice.

She'd taken that final step and could no longer stay with Simon knowing she'd slept with another man. On the computer she left him a typed letter explaining that they just wanted different things. While she wasn't sure what she expected to get from Bernard, she was certain of the way he'd made her feel. For now, that would suffice.

So on Monday she'd walked into her office with a definite pep in her step. That faltered when she'd gotten into her office and listened to her voice mail. There was a message from Simon. Bernard had insisted she get a new cell phone Friday evening, tossing her old one into the trash while they were still in the T-Mobile store. So Simon had no other way of getting in touch with her.

"I got your letter," the message began. "I see you've made up your mind and moved on. There's really not much I can say. I've never been anything but honest with you, Casey. I'm sorry if that wasn't enough. I wish things didn't have to end this way but I understand you have to go for what you want. I hope you find it."

That was it.

Not the reaction she'd expected, but then she hadn't expected him to truly not want to marry her either. Casey sat down at her desk, amazed at how much her life had changed in the span of a week.

Her phone buzzed and she jumped in her seat. Picking it up, she reached over to switch on her computer. "Casey McKnight."

"Hey, sweetie. Just wanted to hear your voice."

It was Bernard.

"You just saw me in the parking lot," she said, smiling. She'd been doing that a lot since Friday.

"I know, but I'm missing you already. How about lunch?"

Casey was typing in passwords and pulling up her e-mails as he talked. "Um, don't know. I've got a ton of messages here that I should really go through. And Diamond took a call from Panzene this morning. They want to see the commercial tomorrow."

"Really? So soon?" Bernard paused. "I didn't hear about that."

"I told her to send an e-mail to your secretary to put on your schedule. It's at ten. Are you looking at your calendar?"

He paused. "I wasn't," he said, then she heard the clicking of his fingers on the keyboard. "Oh, yeah. She put it on there. Have you seen the final version?"

"Not yet. But Jay was going to have a copy hand-delivered to me today."

"Good, we need to get together this afternoon to look at it. I want to be prepared for any questions or issues that might come up tomorrow."

"Okay, that sounds good. We can meet around one."

"We'll order lunch in."

"Sure. Should I send a message to Leonard and Meosha to join in the meeting too?"

Bernard paused again. He'd been remembering more and more about the night in Antigua, the night he'd thought Casey had come to his room. He'd had dinner with Leonard. His so-called friend had been quite comfortable refilling Bernard's glass over and over again. And because Bernard had been tense about his missed shot with Casey he'd been all too willing to ease his lust with liquor.

After that, it was Meosha who had come into his room. Yeah, Bernard had pieced together a lot since Friday. He knew about Lisette hiring Breakdown, Inc. and he'd even sent an e-mail to the notorious Nola Brentwood telling her she could kiss her sweet ass good-bye as well.

"No. I'll call them. Don't worry about it," he told Casey.

He had plans for both Leonard and Meosha. Plans he definitely did not want Casey to know about.

Leonard sat in his office surfing the Net. He'd just come back from Antigua on Saturday. While most of the staff had returned either Thursday or Friday he'd taken another day to enjoy more of the sights.

In actuality he'd enjoyed more of the woman in the room across from his. After his pool antics with Nola he'd been horny for the next available woman. Unfortunately, Ms. Brentwood had made it perfectly clear that she was not that one. Which was cool in his mind. Playing around with a woman as dangerous as Nola wasn't good for his future. So he'd done what she asked as repayment for her doing everything he wanted that afternoon in the pool.

Now he was back to work and wondering where to go from here. Panzene was going to want to see the commercial soon. He hadn't seen it yet but he'd been in close contact with Jay throughout his stay on the island. He wanted to make sure that he knew everything there was to know about the commercial since Bernard was undoubtedly preoccupied.

Subsequently, Leonard would take this opportunity to shine in the next meeting. He'd know things that Bernard didn't, especially since his so-called boss had abruptly left the island on Thursday afternoon. Leonard sensed it had something to do with the disappearance of Casey McKnight, but he didn't pursue the issue. Bernard was doing exactly what Leonard wanted him to do, stepping out of the picture.

So Leonard had arrived in the office early this morning, checked all his e-mails and read over reports on smaller accounts that had been left on his desk over the past week for approval. By nine o'clock he was all caught up and simply waiting for the next assignment. Bernard didn't stroll into the office until just after ten, he and Casey both arriving at the same time.

Leonard could only shake his head when he saw them step off the elevator. When was Bernard going to learn? He suspected his colleague's lesson in love and life was coming sooner rather than later.

He'd been watching a particularly hilarious clip on YouTube when there was a brief knock on his door and then it opened. A quick glance at the computer clock told him it was just minutes before noon. Leonard did a few clicks to clear his computer screen, then sat back in his chair.

"Mornin'," he said with a huge grin. "I see you made it back in one piece."

Bernard didn't smile back, simply closed and locked the door behind him. This wasn't uncommon for him, since he and Leonard usually spent time in the office talking about things that had nothing to do with business and they liked their privacy. So as he moved toward Leonard's desk he watched as the man he'd called his friend leaned casually back in his chair. Carefree and unsuspecting.

"Yeah, I came back early to take care of some business." Bernard thought about taking a seat, then decided against it. What he came to do wouldn't take long.

Leonard nodded. "Some sweet business, I would say. I saw you and Casey arriving together this morning. Shall I venture to say that you finally sealed that deal?"

Bernard was trying valiantly to hold onto his anger. They were still in the office and a big scene was the last thing he wanted. Still, there was no way he could continue to work with Leonard, considering what he'd done to him. Once a colleague and a friend breached that trust there was no going back. So no matter how much Bernard had come to rely on his friendship with Leon-ard, that relationship was over for good. Now he simply needed to sever the ties.

"You stayed in Antigua after I left. Did you enjoy yourself?" Bernard asked, slipping his hands into his pockets.

"Man, those chicks were off the chain. You should have taken an extra day and enjoyed some of them with me. I had a ball."

Bernard nodded. He was sure he had.

"So did you ever hit that Panzene exec? What's her name, Kingsley?"

Leonard straightened his tie, the smile never wavering from his face. "Come on, playa. You know me and you know my game. Of course, I gave honey a little piece."

"And just what did she give you, Leonard?" Bernard asked, feeling a bit of remorse but much more pity for

Leonard. He wondered if the man knew he'd been used and would now suffer the consequences.

"You know, she was just all right, nothing to do cartwheels over. Now, the honey I met at the resort was so much more. Man, she was doing shit I ain't never had done to me before." Leonard tossed his head back as he laughed.

"Was she enough to lose your job over?" Bernard asked seriously.

Leonard immediately sobered, sitting up straighter in his chair. "Why do you ask that?"

"It's simple, that little piece of pussy you just couldn't wait to have just cost you the job you've been working so hard at for ten years."

"What?" Leonard stood. "My job performance has nothing to do with who I fuck. You of all people should know that," he said with more than a hint of sarcasm.

"I thought I knew who I could trust. But apparently pussy is stronger than friendship."

"Man, you never said you were trying to get at Kingsley."

Bernard simply shook his head. "You can cut the act now, Len. I know what you did. I know what she asked you to do. What I don't get is why you did it? I thought you were my man."

"Bernard," Leonard began but Bernard cut him off with sharp shake of his head.

"You paid for pussy by betraying me. That's some ignorant shit, Len. Ignorant and you know it!"

"Wait a minute. You are not seriously going to stand here and talk about betrayal like you're snow-white clean in all this."

Bernard knew Leonard well. He'd known the man wouldn't grovel or beg. He and Leonard were very much alike, when their back was against the wall they came out swinging. Well, that suited him just fine. He'd taken off his suit jacket before going to Len's office because there were just some things a man didn't tolerate, one of which was being set up by his best friend.

"I never sold you out. Would never have done something so dirty."

"But you're dirty enough to fuck around on your wife with every available piece of pussy you can find."

Bernard was startled at Leonard's statement. For years he'd been sharing his sexual exploits with the man. And for years Leonard had seemed just as excited about Bernard's conquests as he did himself. "My wife has nothing to do with what you did."

"No, see, that's where you're wrong. Lisette has everything to do with it."

Leonard had said his wife's name on many occasions in the past years but Bernard was sure he'd never heard it sound quite this way before. "Don't go there, Len. I'm telling you, whatever you're about to say, just don't do it." Anger was boiling in him now, at the new suspicion that had just arisen. Leonard had no idea how close he was coming to being tore the fuck up in this office.

"Don't go there? You mean don't talk about the good woman you have at home while you continue to fuck all these sluts in and out of the office." Leonard pushed his chair back until it slammed against the credenza. "How do you think that makes her feel, Bernard? She knows you're cheating on her. She knows you've always been cheating on her, you arrogant bastard!"

Bernard's voice had lowered to a dangerous level. "How do you know what *my* wife knows, Len? How do you have any idea what she knows and how she feels about it?"

"I'm not stupid and neither is Lisette! Plus, I've been warning her, telling her she needs to leave your sorry ass. She needs to find a man to treat her the way she should be treated."

With each word he spoke Bernard's rage level heightened until his long legs were stepping up onto Leonard's desk, carrying him closer so that when he stepped down, his fist landed with a resounding *crack* over the man's jaw. "That's some real bitch-assness! You've been talking to my wife about me!" he roared, his fist connecting with Leonard's face with each word.

Leonard had fallen back against the credenza with the shock of Bernard's attack. But now that the element of surprise had taken its toll he'd regained some composure and landed a punch just south of Bernard's right eye.

"You're the dumb-ass! She's too good for you. I kept telling her that over and over!"

"Did you touch my wife? You dirty bastard, did you fuck my wife?" Bernard roared, grabbing Leonard by the collar and slamming him against the wall.

Leonard smiled. Even though blood was running from the corner of his mouth and his nose, he smiled. "Lisette's too good to just fuck. So when I get her beneath me you can rest assured I'm going to love her the way your punk ass should have."

Blinded with fury, Bernard kept his handle on Leonard's collar and swung him around until his body slammed into the desk, sliding over it and knocking all the contents to the floor.

There was a hurried knock at the door, bringing Bernard back to the reality that he was at work. He was an executive at CCM and as such this type of behavior did not look well. So straightening his own tie, he moved toward the door, then turned back to look at Leonard, who was struggling to get up from the floor.

"You're done here. Pack up your shit and get out." He reached for the doorknob, then gave Leonard one parting warning. "If I see your face again, or you get within a foot of my wife I'll cut off your balls and feed them to my dog."

Chapter 21

"Are you sure you're okay?" Casey asked Bernard as they sat in his office on Tuesday morning just moments before their scheduled meeting with the Panzene execs.

"I'm fine," he snapped, grabbing his jacket off the back of his chair and standing to put it on.

Casey folded her arms. "Look, I know we've only been together for a couple of days but I'm not stupid. I can see that something's wrong with you. I heard about the fight you had with Leonard yesterday. Is that why you missed our meeting? And why you didn't come back to the apartment until late last night?"

His dark gaze caught hers. "Let it go, Casey."

She looked flabbergasted. "Let it go? Two grown men fistfighting in the office one day, Leonard's gone the next and you want me to forget it? How do we explain to the Panzene execs that one of our team is gone?"

"We say he got fired. Poor work performance. CCM is our company, Panzene has no say over who stays and who goes."

"And who has that say, Bernard? Because you know Meosha didn't come to work yesterday and I stopped by her office this morning and she's not in today. Her secretary hasn't seen or heard from her. So the team is down two members. Do you know where she is?"

"No, I don't know where that trick is!" he yelled.

Again, Casey stared at him as if she had no idea who he was. "Tell me what's going on."

Running a hand down his face, Bernard moved to stand beside Casey. He took a couple deep, steadying breaths before speaking. "Look, I'm sorry I'm in such a crappy mood. It's the divorce with Lisette. She's not letting me see Madison and she's making outrageous demands. It's just got me stressed-out."

"That's not why you were fighting with Leonard."

Bernard sighed. "Look, Casey, what happened between me and Leonard is personal, it wasn't business."

"Then he shouldn't have been fired."

"He was fired because he let his personal feelings get in the way of our business deal. He made a poor decision that could have cost us the Panzene account, but more importantly cost us our friendship. Now even though that decision was a personal one, I cannot tolerate someone being that stupid as to jeopardize everything that I've worked for."

She was still eyeing him suspiciously. "Everything that *we've* worked for," she said slowly.

Bernard gave her a small smile, then pulled her closer. "That's right, baby. Everything we've worked for. He was an idiot, so I got rid of him."

"And Meosha?"

"I honestly don't know where she is, but if she's AWOL, she's going to lose her job as well. I don't have time for games when there's a multimillion-dollar deal on the table. Understand?"

Casey nodded. He was touching her, so all coherent thought was fleeing her mind. When he touched his lips lightly to hers she all but melted in his arms.

"You need to relax. The commercial is going to be great. Panzene will love it and they'll love you for heading up the team that came up with it. Everything will work out just fine, you'll see."

Bernard heard her words and felt relieved to have her on his side. Last night had been tumultuous at best. He'd known Meosha wasn't in the office because he'd gone looking for her soon after his altercation with Leonard. He wanted both of them out of his firm. But she hadn't been there. He'd called her house and her cell phone and hadn't gotten in contact with her. Finding out that she wasn't in this morning was a bit disconcerting but slightly relieving. He wouldn't have to deal with her today.

Hopefully, she'd been paid enough money from Nola Brentwood to leave town for good. That scenario would suit him even better. But for now, they had a meeting to go to, a deal to seal and then a future to plan.

Around the conference room table Jay, the producer, Corbin Censor, and a woman Bernard had just informed Casey was Emile Jennings from Panzene, were already seated.

In addition to wondering where Meosha was, Casey had questioned Bernard about Kingsley as well. The question had been dismissed as they walked into the conference room, greeting everyone already inside and taking a seat at the long cherrywood table.

Casey sat in the leather-backed executive chair, dropping her file, the case with her reading glasses inside, and her pen on the table. She'd worn a dark blue pantsuit but decided that with her nerves on overload she needed to remove the jacket. So she placed it on the back of her chair before sitting down.

To her right was Emile Jennings from Panzene, a middle-aged white woman with glossy gray eyes and skin that had frequented the tanning salons a bit too much. Her hair was a chalky blond with darker roots battling for superiority. She extended a hand to Casey as she took her seat but her greeting didn't ring sincere. Casey had been in the world of business long enough not to expect much more.

Corbin smiled at her from the opposite side of the table and Casey watched Bernard take his seat right next to him.

"Is this all of us?" Corbin asked.

For a moment Casey tensed, wondering how Bernard was ultimately going to explain Leonard and Meosha's absence.

"Yes. We can meet about the others reassignment afterward," Bernard answered smoothly, giving Casey a quick glance.

"Great. Let's get started." Jay reached over the table, snagging up the slim black remote control that operated the DVD player that had been set up on the credenza at the far end of the room.

It was then that Casey noted the projector screen that extended from the tiles in the ceiling. She stood quickly, touching the panel that electronically closed the blinds on the extensive view of the other buildings occupying Pratt Street. The room darkened substantially, but that was okay since the blue light from the DVD player's information screen now illuminated the room.

Just as Casey returned to her seat a cone of light fell across the conference room table and all heads turned to the opening door. Casey's mouth gaped as she watched Lisette Williamson walk through the door. She'd never met the woman but she'd seen pictures of her in the paper, in magazines, and the one small photo of her and his daughter that Bernard kept on the book stand in his office.

Her gaze flew instantly to him.

Bernard's jaw clenched but Casey doubted anyone but her had seen it. Instead, he stood, going to his wife, taking her elbow in his hand and leaning forward to whisper something in her ear.

Lisette was beautiful with her long auburn hair reaching past her shoulders, her honey-toned skin perfectly highlighted by the pewter-colored skirt and jacket she wore. Her makeup was impeccable, natural looking but sophisticated at the same time. Casey felt a slight pang of jealousy at the way Bernard seemed right at home standing next to her.

"Lisette, I'm glad you could join us," Emile said, standing on Casey's other side. "Here's a seat right here. Come on over so we can get started."

At the woman's voice, Bernard turned to her. "I apologize for the intrusion but my wife is not on this team."

"Of course she's not," Emile said with a smile. "She's on the Panzene board, that's why she's here."

Bernard shot an annoyed glance at Lisette, who only smiled as she moved easily out of his grasp, walking toward the empty seat left next to Casey.

Casey's heart thumped and she flattened her hands on the table in an attempt to steady her breathing.

"Corbin, you remember Lisette, don't you?" Emile asked when Lisette put her purse on the table and pulled out the chair to sit.

"I do. It's been a long time since I've seen her. But it's always a pleasure," Corbin said, standing to reach out and shake her hand.

"Same here," Lisette said and Casey cringed at her

throaty voice. It suited her perfectly, giving her an air of allure to go with her astonishing beauty.

"This is Jay Wintro, he's the producer of the masterpiece we're about to unveil," Censor said, motioning toward Jay, who quickly stood to shake Lisette's hand as well.

"I apologize for being late. I had to get little Madison settled first. She missed her daddy this morning," Lisette said, tossing a sickeningly sweet smile over to Bernard.

Casey raised a brow toward Bernard, who had already sat back in his seat. When he caught her glance he cleared his throat. "Lisette, this is Casey McKnight. She's the junior exec who came up with the idea for the commercial."

Then Lisette turned her full attention on Casey. The woman's long legs lowered her to the seat as she extended a hand. Casey mustered up her best professional smile and met her hand halfway. "It's nice to meet you," she said.

Lisette nodded her head, shimmering locks of hair sliding sensually to the side as she gave Casey a cross between a smile and smirk. "The pleasure is all mine."

Oh God, did she know Casey was now sleeping with her husband? Casey desperately hoped not. Bernard said they were separated. Still, Casey didn't want the drama of a confrontation with her lover's wife, even if Lisette looked way too classy to stoop to making a scene in the middle of a meeting.

"All right, let's get this show on the road. I'm too excited about this to wait another minute," Jay said as he moved to close the door.

His right arm was extended toward the screen as Casey presumed he pressed play. They all waited with bated breath as the screen turned black then brightened with aerial shots of Antigua.

The background music was a smooth mixture of Island jingle with hip-hop bass that gave a fun, contemporary appeal. Casey sat back in her chair, swiveling on the wheeled base so that her back was completely to Lisette. She watched with her complete focus on the screen. The music was one of the last things she and Jay had discussed before she'd left the island. She was pleased with his final choice.

Bernard divided his attention between the screen and his wife. What the hell was she doing here? And when did she acquire enough stock to sit on Panzene's board of directors? Apparently she'd been much more into the business than Bernard had ever considered.

That still didn't explain why she was here, now. He hadn't spoken to her since Sunday morning when she'd called, asking him if he were staying in his apartment. Bernard hadn't been surprised that she'd found about the apartment. If she'd had enough gumption to hire Nola Brentwood, clearly she was out to find all the dirt on him she could.

Fortunately, Lisette knew she'd never be a match for him. She'd tried to echo the threat that Brentwood had given him the day before, but he'd quickly shut her down.

"If you continue I'll fight for full custody of Madison. Then you'll be completely alone. Think about what you're doing, Lisette. You know you can't win."

"I don't want to win, Bernard," she'd told him. "It's apparent that there will be no winners in this situation. I just want my due."

"I don't owe you anything," he said quickly.

"You owe me everything. I've been your loyal and devoted wife for seven years. I gave you a beautiful child, I've stood by your side while you've climbed the corporate ladder. And let's not forget that when you walk into city hall as the next city councilman, it'll be because of my father."

"Wives are a dime a dozen. And this loyalty you're spouting is a joke. If you were so loyal you wouldn't have gone to an outsider to negotiate our private matters."

"If you were any kind of man you wouldn't have gone to all those other women!" she'd yelled on the other end of the phone.

"You knew I never loved you," he said finally. He'd never told her that, never mentioned that she'd trapped him into marriage.

"When you married me, you made a commitment. You had a responsibility to me and to Madison."

"Madison is my child. I know my responsibility to her and will honor it till the day I die. You, on the other hand, are nothing."

She'd grown quiet at that comment, then said in a voice not much above a whisper, "I'm glad I finally know where I stand with you."

"Whatever. Look, I don't have time for this right now. I'll have my attorney draw up the papers. You'll be taken care of, don't worry. Madison is a given, whatever she wants or needs I'll take care of. You can have the house and your car and one of the bank accounts."

"It's not about money," she'd responded.

"That's all there is between us, Lisette. That's all there's ever been. When you get an attorney to represent you instead of that criminal Brentwood, call my secretary with the name and number. I'll have my attorney get in touch with him with the details. Oh, and I'll be by later today to see Madison."

She'd hung up the phone then and lowered her head into her hands. She wanted to cry, actually prayed for the tears to come, but in their place was anger. Boiling deep in the pit of her stomach, hot and fierce, was the pain and embarrassment that Bernard had brought into her life. For endless moments it made its home in her body, circulating until she shivered with its darkness filtering through her.

In that moment she knew she hated him, wanted to hurt him as badly as he'd hurt her.

Finally, the voice whispered in her head and this time she didn't try to shake it away.

Bernard was remembering the same exchange between him and Lisette. He'd disconnected the phone after telling her that he was coming to see Madison because the timid and confused Lisette had remained quiet. So saying it was a shock to see her walk into this meeting today was an understatement. She hadn't been at the house when he'd arrived Saturday afternoon to see Madison. And he hadn't heard from her since then. Now she sat across the table as if she were totally interested in seeing this commercial. Bernard knew she had to be up to something and if he found out that it was at the instruction of Nola Brentwood, they were both going to pay dearly.

The lighting changed in the room, drawing Bernard's attention back to the screen. They were on the white sand beach of Rendezvous Bay now, the sapphire blue water crashing in slight waves against the jagged rocks of the cliff. The music had switched to a sultry rhythm, then Georgette and Shai had appeared, laying on the sand, bodies entwined.

The narration was read by R&B recording star Sebastian Simpson. His voice was smooth, romantic, and sexy, according to Casey and Meosha, who had rallied hard to get him on board. Bernard had to admit that the voice was a perfect overlay to the beach backdrop and the sexiness of the couple on the screen. There was a close-up of Georgette's face that was meant to highlight the naturally seductive look of Panzene's cosmetics.

Georgette played her role well, staring alluringly into the camera. Shai's hands roamed Georgette's perfectly toned body. The camera slid from Georgette's face, down the length of their bodies, until the only thing on the screen were entwined legs, Georgette's darker ones with Shai's slightly lighter ones.

As they'd planned, the lighting flashed over Georgette's skin, displaying perfectly the barely there foundation, the shimmering smooth eye shadow and the glossy and alluring lip gloss. Panzene's Seductive products were excellently displayed. Georgette's natural beauty only highlighting the cosmetics.

Shai did his job well, touching Georgette, looking at her as if she were the most beautiful woman in the world. All the while the palm trees and white sand beaches gave an air of romance, a whimsical allure to the term *seduction*.

Then nightfall covered the screen. They were moving to the shots of Georgette and Shai having dinner at a terrace restaurant, the beach a backdrop to their candlelight dinner. Or so that was what the scene was supposed to show. Instead, shots of the Horizon appeared, then the bubbling jets of a Jacuzzi. For one long moment Bernard's chest clenched. It was the spa room that he and Casey were in, he had no doubt. The camera had panned the room and his room key and cell phone sat on the table nearest the door. The screen continued to display the room from the patio to the candles lit all along the interior. When it fell on the Jacuzzi it was empty. Thankfully.

Bernard remembered the picture he'd received of he and Casey in that very room and looked over at her to see if she remembered as well. But she was staring at the screen, her legs crossed, her back firmly pressed against the chair.

A glance at Lisette and his gut clenched again. She wasn't smiling and she wasn't looking at the screen. She was looking at Casey. Her eyes glazed, her brow knotted. Her chest heaved as she looked to be trying to control her temper, and slowly but surely losing the battle.

There was a ringing sound and Bernard once again turned his attention to the screen. On the table in the spa the camera had a close-up on his cell phone as it rang. The caller ID screen illuminated blue and read *unavailable*. Bernard frowned, remembering he'd received an unavailable call while in the spa. He shifted uncomfortably, knowing instinctively this wasn't a coincidence.

Bernard sat forward in his chair, his hand inching across the table to the remote Jay had left in the middle of the table. Something was definitely going on here and he didn't like it. Lisette's appearance at the meeting, the fact that she'd hired Nola Brentwood—who upon further investigation had come across her notorious reputation when a tape was played of Nola and her cousin's fiancé having sex at a family gathering—coupled with Nola's threats and his final words to Lisette two days ago, all rattled through his mind.

He needed to stop this before it got way out of hand. But just as he felt the edge of the remote in his hand the scene changed. The room was dimly lit; a blurred shot of the dresser filled with Panzene products appeared. The shot spanned out, catching the edge of the bed, the floral comforter that had been on all the beds at the Horizon, then a bare ankle, a woman's ankle.

The room was suddenly hot, Bernard's head pounding as he closed his fingers around the remote and pulled it closer to him.

The female ankles no longer occupied the screen. Now the shot cleared significantly to capture a round mocha-colored ass. The first gasp came from Emile.

Bernard hurriedly pushed a button. It fast-forwarded to the next scene.

It was of Meosha's face contorted with ecstasy.

"What the—" Censor murmured.

Again Bernard pushed buttons on the remote and again the scene fast-forwarded.

This time it filled with his face, his hands grasping plump breasts, pulling them into his mouth. "Fuck!" he yelled and stood up pointing the remote at the screen and pressing all the buttons he could at one time.

Across the table he heard Casey gasp.

On the screen the scene panned out so that not only was he shown sucking some blond chick's tits but that Meosha was now quite clearly riding his cock.

"*Daayyuuuummm,*" Jay roared.

"What the hell is this?" Emile yelled. "This isn't the commercial we paid for. This is lewd and unacceptable!"

Casey swiveled in her chair, her gaze landing solidly on Bernard.

"Get the lights on," Censor spoke loudly. "And turn this shit off!"

The room seemed to be spinning as Bernard finally found the stop button and the screen went blank. Simultaneously, the lights came on and his gaze flew to Lisette.

Like a scene in slow motion he watched as his wife moved forward in her chair, reaching an arm toward Casey. Casey had been staring at him and had no clue what Lisette was doing but as the blinds at the window behind them slipped open the rays of the sun caught the gleam of metal just seconds before Lisette jabbed the blade into Casey's side.

Casey screamed, hunching over in her chair. Bernard

pushed his chair back and attempted to climb over the conference-room table to get to Casey when Lisette pulled the knife out of her side, then grabbed Casey in a headlock, pulling her up out of the chair.

"Get the hell back!" she told Bernard, holding Casey with one arm and brandishing the bloodstained knife with the other.

Bernard paused. Emile scrambled to get around to the other side of the table, away from Lisette.

"What do you think you're doing?"

"Lisette, what's gotten into you?"

Bernard and Censor spoke at the same time. Lisette was shaking her head, her eyes wild, the hand that held the knife shaking.

This wasn't the soft-spoken woman he'd married, Bernard thought suddenly. She looked totally different, sounded strange, crazy or deranged. Either-or didn't seem to accurately explain the situation he now faced.

"You're fucking her now! She's the flavor of the month!" Lisette spat. "Don't try to deny it. I saw you. At your apartment I saw you with her!"

Bernard was smart enough not to even attempt denial. The knife was dangerously close to Casey's neck now, its bloodstained tip ready to sink into her flesh once more. "Lisette, come on, we talked about this the other day. Our marriage is over." He spoke in a voice as calmly as he could muster. He tried not to look directly at Casey, although her fear reached across the room to claw at him fiercely.

"You're damned right it's over! All of it is over!" Moving her hand down, she jammed the knife into Casey's side again. Her eyes glistened as she sunk the blade into Casey's flesh and when she pulled it out her lips spread in an evil grin that chilled Bernard down to his toes.

"No!" Bernard yelled and finished his descent over the

table, coming to stand right beside Lisette. He was holding his hands in front of him, reaching out to her. "Stop! Stop! It isn't worth it. I'm not worth it," he told her. "Let Casey go and we'll talk."

Lisette was shaking her head now, her shoulder-length auburn hair swishing wildly. "Talking's over, isn't that what you told me the other day?"

Even her voice was different, huskier, filled with a hatred he hadn't detected until this point. He couldn't believe this was happening. Casey was bleeding, the front of her white blouse now stained with blood. She was heaving, struggling to breathe, her eyes rolling in the back of her head.

"Lisette, think about what you're doing. Think about Madison. Put the knife down and we'll go someplace to talk. You don't want to do this." He was desperate, saying whatever was absolutely necessary to get Lisette to stop before she . . . he couldn't even think it.

"It hurts, Bernard," Casey whispered. She was pale now, her dark hair wildly framing her beautiful face.

Her words gripped his heart and Bernard wanted to cry out. Instead, he tried to steady his own breathing. "I know. Just stay calm," he told her.

"Stay calm! What the fuck!" Lisette roared. "You're still more worried about this slut than you are me. I'm your wife, Bernard!" she screamed, the knife shaking in her hand even as tears streamed down her face.

"I know! I know who you are, Lisette. I just need you to let her go. Right now, just let Casey go."

"Hell no! She needs to be taught a lesson too!" Lisette looked down at Casey, who was barely standing now, her weakness threatening to pull both of them down. "You can't fuck other women's husbands!" Lisette yelled at her, then touched the knife to her temple. "No matter how pretty you are."

"No!" Bernard screamed and lunged at Lisette.

But Lisette was faster, the voice in her head yelling, "Do it! Do it!"

The knife bit into Casey's tender flesh, ripping a jagged line down her cheek, stopping at her jaw when Bernard's body crashed into Lisette's, knocking the three of them to the floor.

Nola stared at the screen in horrified shock. The events playing out before her were too miserable to believe. Jay, who she recognized as the producer of the commercial was yelling for someone to call 911, while the Panzene rep, Emile, screamed and covered her face as Corbin folded her into his arms, turning her away from the gruesome scene.

She'd installed a tiny camera in the front of the conference room earlier this morning when she'd snuck into CCM's offices. As an extra incentive, Breakdown, Inc. always provided a copy of the actual breakdown to their clients. So she'd been recording and watching from an empty office on the fifth floor of the building that CCM was in.

Seeing Lisette walk in had alarmed Nola. The look on Lisette's face had confirmed the niggling feelings she'd had yesterday after Lisette had left her office. The woman just hadn't looked right. Her reaction to what Nola was telling her hadn't seemed right. She was off in some way that Nola hadn't noticed before. She wished like hell she'd noticed before.

Nola couldn't have known it would end this way. She couldn't have stopped it, she steadily tried to convince herself. Her fingers were nervously dialing Gee's cell phone even as she kept her eyes glued to the screen.

Bernard was pushing Lisette off of Casey, who was now bleeding profusely.

"Call nine-one-one!" His voice echoed through the screen to fill the small room Nola was in as he leaned over Casey, cupping her face in his hands, whispering soft words to her.

Lisette stood perfectly still, knife in hand. She was looking at Bernard as if she were trying to figure out what to do next. Nobody in the room dared to touch her but Nola sensed she'd already done what she came to do.

"Gee! Gee! She's going to kill him! I'm watching Lisette kill her husband!" Nola yelled the instant Gee answered his phone. Why she'd called him first she had no idea. Then again, she did. Since the confrontation in her office she and Gee had talked a lot about her business, the direction it would take from this point on and their life together.

Gee was in her corner, he wanted to be there for her and Nola finally admitted that at this stage in her life, it would be nice to have someone she could lean on.

"What? Nola? Where are you?"

"I'm downtown," she panted. "At the CCM building. I was on the fifth floor taping the breakdown and Lisette is going off. She's stabbing people and there's so much blood and—and—I can't breathe!" Nola screamed.

She hadn't anticipated this and for as much as she'd held a gun on a man she'd never witnessed such brutality as she was seeing now. The room seemed to be spinning around her as Casey and Bernard's screams echoed in her head.

"Don't move! Don't you fucking move! I'm on my way," Gee yelled into the phone.

"You son of a bitch!" Lisette was screaming from the screen now, coming out of the trance Nola had just witnessed a few seconds ago.

"No," Nola whispered, knowing there was no way the woman could hear her. "No, Lisette. He's not worth it."

Nola was shaking her head but knew there was no way she could stop what was about to happen.

"You're my husband! You're supposed to love *me!*" Lisette continued. Her fingers clamped around the knife, her eyes wild, tears streaming down her face. "You're supposed to love me," she whimpered a second before lifting the arm that held the knife and bringing the bloodied blade down, thrusting sharply into her stomach.

"You're supposed to love me," she said again, pulled the knife out and jabbed it into herself once more. "Just me," she stuttered and stabbed herself again.

Jay finally uprooted himself from where he'd stood by the door, rushing across the room to grab Lisette's arm before she could insert the knife again.

Hot tears tracked Nola's cheeks as she watched Lisette's slim form slip to the floor, Jay catching her in his arms.

Chapter 22

"The plastic surgeon will see her some time tomorrow after some of the swelling has gone down," Dr. Alegra Palmer told Simon as they stood outside of the hospital room. "The surgery went well and she's stable right now. You can see her for a few minutes then the staff needs to prepare her to be moved to a room on the floor."

Simon nodded his head, giving a silent thanks to God that Casey was going to be okay.

The television in the apartment had been on as he'd stepped out of the shower earlier today. He'd heard bits and pieces while he dressed of some hostage standoff in a downtown office building. But it was when he'd sat on the edge of the bed to put on his shoes that he'd glanced at the screen.

The picture from her driver's license appeared. Casey. His Casey. "One person gravely wounded, Casey McKnight, a junior executive at Censor Creative Media. And another pronounced dead at the scene, Lisette Cheyenne

Williamson, wife of Censor VP Bernard Williamson, in what looks like a lovers' triangle turned deadly. I'm Denise Mitchell reporting for Action News."

His heart had simply stopped beating. Casey was hurt. Operating on pure adrenaline from that point on Simon had raced to the University of Maryland Shock Trauma in search of the woman he loved. He wasn't surprised that he was the only person there for Casey. Her parents lived in Pennsylvania and they rarely talked. For the past five years, he'd been all she had.

And she'd been all he had, all he'd ever wanted. The thought that she might die clawed at him with a vicious intensity. Simon sat in the waiting room, his hands sweating, his mind reeling with what-ifs. If he'd just agreed to marry her, all this could have been prevented.

Yet, he'd had his reasons for not doing that and Casey wasn't a stranger to any of them. His parents had a horrible marriage and an even more horrendous divorce. He didn't want to walk that road. Even now one of his sisters was going through a messy divorce of her own. Simon had liked things the way they were with Casey. They were in love and committed to each other, that should have been all that mattered.

But to Casey it wasn't.

He'd let her go because that's what she'd wanted. He'd thought about chasing her, begging her, but then he'd be asking her to settle for something she no longer wanted. That would have been selfish and he couldn't stand doing that to her.

Now she was here in the hospital, fighting for her life and he felt like a complete idiot. He should have called her, should have spoken to her personally, told her that he loved her and he'd do anything to keep her, to make her happy.

But was that the truth? Was he willing to marry her

even though the thought of such a union scared him shit-less?

"Recovery isn't going to be easy," Dr. Palmer contin-ued. "She's going to need a lot of moral support. The in-juries to her face were extensive, not to mention the perforated lung."

Simon nodded. "I understand. I'll be here for her," he promised the woman he didn't even know when he should have been promising to Casey. "I'm going to see her now."

Dr. Palmer simply nodded and Simon stepped closer to the door of the room where Casey was. He paused, took a deep breath, and then opened the door.

She looked so small in the big bed. All those white sheets and the white bandages wrapped tightly around her head and down the side of her face made her look pale. Tears stung Simon's eyes as he approached.

Instantly he reached for her hand that lay so still at her side, tracked with IVs and surgical tape. She felt cold. He jumped at the incessant beeping from all the machines surrounding her bed.

"Casey," he said on a choked cry. "I'm here, baby. I'm right here and I'm not going to let you go, not ever again."

"What the fuck are you doing here?" Bernard asked when he'd used the key to enter the house he'd shared with Lisette.

After the police had finished questioning him he'd gone straight there. He'd needed to see Madison. To hold her close and know that she was safe.

"That doesn't matter."

"The hell it doesn't. Where's Madison?"

Leonard shook his head. "She's no longer your con-cern."

"Man, fuck you! Where's my daugher?" Bernard charged Leonard, only to be pushed back with such force that he stumbled backward, his ass hitting the floor with brutal force.

"She's gone!"

"Gone? Where?"

"You don't give a damn," Leonard spat. "You never did. You had it all and you fucked around until you lost it! Lisette's gone because of you, now you won't get your hands on her daughter."

"Madison is my daughter! And Lisette did exactly what she wanted to do. I didn't kill her!"

"No. Your lying and cheating killed her just the same as if you'd stabbed her yourself. Why couldn't you be man enough to leave her if you didn't want her." Leonard's voice hitched, his eyes filling with tears as he stepped toward Bernard.

This was the man he'd thought was his friend, his confidant. Bernard had spent the better part of the last day thinking about Leonard and how he'd betrayed him by harboring feelings for Lisette. A friend didn't fall for another man's wife. But Leonard had and now Bernard was face-to-face with the extent of Leonard's feelings for his dead wife. Getting up from the floor, Bernard was about to take another swing at him, angered at the situation with his friend and Lisette, the fact that Casey now lay in a hospital bed and the knowledge that his daughter was somewhere without him, pissing him off to the point he needed to hit somebody. But he stopped short when Leonard reached into his jacket and pulled out a gun.

His hand shook as he aimed and put his finger directly on the trigger. "I told you she deserved better. She deserved me. And now . . . now, you deserve to die!" Leonard said solemnly.

"No," Bernard said simply. His head was roaring, his

stomach twisting in knots that threatened to uncurl with waves of intense nausea. "This is not happening. I need Madison. Where is Madison?" All he could think about now as he stared at the gun in the hands of the man who was most likely hurting, obviously to the point that he wanted to kill, was his daughter. The little girl that was the light of his life, his reason for enduring the years of unhappiness for as long as he did.

"You're not going to see her again."

Bernard was dizzy, the events of the day rushing through his mind like a summer storm. He stumbled backward again, connecting with the wall in the hallway. "I need to see my daughter." That's all he'd been able to think about. From the moment he'd watched Lisette stabbing Casey, to the seconds just before she'd turned the knife on herself, jabbing it repeatedly into her stomach. Everything he'd done and said from the moment she'd appeared at the door of his dorm room can swirling back.

The night he'd first had sex with her, the day she told him she was pregnant, their wedding night, the night Madison was born, that first woman he'd fucked in the back of his car and each woman after that. The voices had resounded in his head like a sick litany. He'd driven here like a madman trying to run from the past, to get a grip on the present and hopefully to preserve the future.

"I need to see her, just one last time. Please," he begged.

"Too late. You should have thought about her a long time ago. You should have thought about somebody other than yourself." Leonard had been moving toward Bernard as he spoke until now he was right up on him.

"I love my daughter. Please, man." The plea died on Bernard's lips as the cool nozzle of the gun touched his pounding temple and exploded.

Chapter 23

The ride was smooth as Nola sat in the passenger-side seat of Gee's Lexus LX. Her head throbbed, but Gee had reclined the seat the moment she climbed in, so she kept her eyes closed and tried to ignore the images running through her mind like a horrific slide show.

Had she created this situation? Had she pushed Lisette Williamson over the edge? No, her rational mind answered. Whatever was wrong with Lisette had been there long before Nola had entered the picture. Most women who came to her were at their wit's end when it came to figuring out how to deal with their cheating men. Lisette had been way beyond that point, Nola just hadn't seen it.

Her breathing had finally steadied to a normal pace after Gee had hustled her out the small office and into the freight elevator, which led them to the basement of the building. From there they'd moved quickly out a back exit that emptied them into the alleyway between Lombard and Pratt Streets where his SUV was already parked. All around she heard the sirens—police cars and medical services, no doubt. News crews would be on their way, the building secured as a crime scene, a crime she had a part in.

"You think I should have done something different?" she asked Gee quietly.

His answer was swift. "I think that woman had a screw loose from the beginning."

They were speeding along Route 50, heading toward the Chesapeake Bay Bridge. He hadn't said much since busting through the door of the office building and effectively shutting down all her equipment, tossing it into her box and getting her the hell out of there. Nola wondered what he was thinking. For the first time in her life, she actually cared what a man was thinking about her.

"But you never agreed with me opening Breakdown."

"I didn't," he said through gritted teeth. "But I recognized it was something you needed to do so I backed off."

"You don't understand it," she said simply, turning her head so that she could look at him. He was dressed in his correctional officer uniform, his strong hands gripping the steering wheel as he stared straight ahead.

"I understand revenge," he said after a few minutes. "I've felt the need for it on more than one occasion. But like we discussed the other day in your office, I don't want you putting yourself in danger. You've got to figure out a way to do your job, to help these women without getting personally involved."

She sighed. "I know, you don't want me sleeping with the clients or their husbands. We've gone over this." She couldn't believe after all this he was still on the sex-with-Meosha thing.

But then he grabbed her arm, squeezing with more strength then he'd ever had. "It's not just about the sex, Nola. It's about your life!"

"I can take care—" The words abruptly halted on her tongue.

"I know, you think you can take care of yourself. You've been doing it so long you don't know how to let somebody else take some of the weight off. But I'm here now and that's exactly what I'm going to do."

"I'm not closing my business," she said adamantly when he'd finally released her arm. They were driving onto the bridge now. The sun was setting, casting an eerie orange glaze over the water below. How many times had she crossed this bridge, how many times had she been so fed up with city life that she'd come home? Funny that Gee would bring her here now.

She'd never thought to invite him home to meet her mother and the rest of her family. But that's because she'd never thought of Gee being a permanent part in her life. As weird as it may have sounded, this case with Bernard and Lisette Williamson may have been the eye-opener she needed. Life was short, especially when you let its circumstances drive you crazy the way Lisette surely had.

Did she have that kind of time to waste? And should she continue wasting it on the memory of what her fa-ther—no, on what Frank Brentwood had done? Hell no! She'd given him enough, enough years, enough tears, enough anger. Now it was time she gave herself something in return.

"It's okay, baby. Everything's going to be okay," Gee whispered to Nola as they lay on a bed at the Whispering Sea Resort in St. Michaels.

For the first time in the fifteen months he'd known her, she'd opened up to him. After arriving at the resort and both of them climbing into the shower together she'd come out and sat on the bed. She didn't look at him when she called him to sit beside her.

Gee didn't question, just went to her, wrapping one arm around her shoulder, taking her hand with the other. She took a deep breath and spoke in a voice that was almost too low for him to hear.

"I've been really angry for a long time at every man that crossed my path. I know now—well, I guess I knew it then but was too stubborn to care—that I was really only pissed at one man. My father."

"Tell me about him," Gee said, brushing a kiss over her forehead.

"He left my mother when I was three years old. Just packed his stuff and walked out. We haven't seen or heard from him since." She finally looked up at him. "I blamed every man that I've met since then for his stupidity. So now, I'm apologizing to you for being so ignorant and so stubborn."

"I don't want your apologies for something as natural as pain and anger. And for the record, I think you've channeled that anger into something really important. Breakdown has a good concept, we just need to work on your execution."

She smiled then and Gee's heart swelled for love for this woman and all she'd been through.

They'd made love then, a slow and sweet culmination that still held the intense edge that would probably never subside between him and Nola and as the night had completely blanketed the sky she'd begun to cry.

He suspected the tears were a long time coming, a purging of her soul that when she finished would give her the fresh outlook she no doubt needed. So Gee simply held her, letting the events of the day replay in his mind even as he knew they were embarking on a new future, together.

When he'd arrived at the office building he'd found her crumpled on the floor, crying hysterically. The camera in the office was still taping so he could clearly see the police moving about, questioning Bernard Williamson and the other people he suspected had been in the room when everything had gone down.

A body had been carried out of the front door on a stretcher when he'd made his way into the building. He hadn't stopped to investigate, simply headed to the elevators, to Nola.

On some level she'd blamed herself for what had happened and while Gee didn't agree with her, he figured it might be a catalyst to her handling the business at Breakdown in a smarter manner. He had some ideas himself but would wait a couple of days before springing them on her.

While he'd been at her office the other day he'd noticed a folder with a name that was all too familiar to him. If she'd taken that case—which, if he knew Nola the way he thought he did, she had—she was going to need his help. Even if she didn't think she needed his help, he was going to give it to her. She was his now and his number-one goal was to protect her, always.

That would be the reason he didn't take her to the hospital when he first picked her up even though he knew she was in a state of shock after what she'd seen. He hadn't wanted to risk her being implicated in this mess. A part of Gee knew it was inevitable, it would definitely come out that Nola had been hired by Lisette Williamson. Once again, Nola would be investigated by the police. The difference this time would be that he had the inside track. He knew officers on the police force and many of them owed him big-time.

But Gee couldn't think about that now. Now, his only concern was keeping Nola safe. Her cell phone had been ringing incessantly when he got to her and he'd seen that it was her cousin Cally calling.

"Take her home," Cally had told him when he answered. "Serena and I will be there as soon as we can."

He'd agreed because he had no idea what else to do with her. "Not to her mother's. I don't want her to see Nola this way," Gee had said.

"You're right. Find a hotel and call me back with the name. I'm going to call Serena now."

"Fine."

"And Gee," Cally added before he could hang up.

"Yeah?"

"Thanks for being there for her. I mean, thanks for loving her."

He did love her, there was no doubt about that and he would protect her with his life. With the business she was in, he had no choice. Emotions ran high where infidelity was concerned. And there was always the chance that these situations could end like this one had or even worse, with Nola's death.

That thought led him to another matter that he'd been meaning to clear up today. As Nola moaned in his arms, her crying finally over as she fell into a fitful slumber, he slipped off the bed, then moved into the bathroom, grabbing his cell phone from the nightstand as he went.

"Yeah?" Cam answered on the second ring.

"Where's the bitch?" Gee asked instantly.

"Still locked in the room at the motel."

"I thought you were moving her out of the city?"

"I am. I needed a few things in place first, but I'm working on it."

"Don't work on it. I want her gone now. For good!"

"What's going on?" Cam asked. "I see there's a lot of shit going on downtown. You hooked up in that?"

"I wasn't but now I am. Nola's client went ballistic,

stabbing up people and whatnot. Look, Meosha's on that tape. They might look for her so I want her gone. I don't want her mentioning that Nola was on the tape too."

"She was?" Cam asked, surprised.

"Stop asking questions and get it done!"

"Yeah. Okay. I'll take care of her tonight."

"Call me when it's finished."

"Will do."

Gee slammed his phone shut and went back out, climbing into the bed and folding Nola into his arms once more.

"It's all right, baby. Nobody's going to hurt you ever again."

It was a little past midnight when Kalita heard the key in the front door. Meosha hadn't come back, but then she'd known she wouldn't. Meosha could hold a grudge longer than anyone Kalita knew. And since she thought Kalita had wronged her, that grudge would last for years and years to come.

A part of Kalita mourned the friendship, while another part accepted the friendship could never have really been if Meosha believed she'd sleep with Cam. That had baffled both Kalita and Cam since Meosha had made it perfectly clear the day Cam had been locked up that she didn't want anything else to do with him. Testifying the way she had, ensuring that Cam would get jail time, was even more evidence to the fact that Meosha considered the relationship with Cam over.

So why was she tripping now?

Sure, there was the code that once a friend slept with a guy, he was off-limits to any other friend. But Kalita thought that was mighty hypocritical of Meosha since she was now in the habit of sleeping with married men. While Meosha wasn't personal friends with the wives of the husbands she slept with, the whole setup was still scandalous.

Just like the dream she'd had about actually sleeping with Cam last night was. Kalita had awakened this morning struggling with guilt until she'd walked into the kitchen and seen Cam fixing a bowl of cereal. He'd been wearing basketball shorts and nothing else. Her mouth had immediately gone dry, the guilt slipping to the back of her mind to be replaced by a lust so potent it almost choked her.

Now, she sat on the couch watching in amazement as the local news covered all the drama that had gone down on Meosha's job. All her life drama seemed to follow Meosha, so Kalita wondered if she were involved.

"Hey?" she said when Cam had come in, slipped the locks into place and put his key in the tray on the table by the door. He was still staying at the condo with her and had even given her a thousand dollars to go toward next month's bills. She knew she should have asked where he'd gotten the money, especially since as far as she knew he didn't have a job, but she didn't. She was just glad to have a man keeping his word and pitching in to help for a change.

"Hey. What are you doing still up on a weeknight? You know you've got to get up early for work tomorrow."

"I know." She moved aside as he sat on the sofa beside her. "Did you hear about what happened at CCM? I wonder if Meosha was there?"

Cam shrugged. "I heard bits and pieces on the radio."

"Hmmm," Kalita said. For all that he'd shown up at her doorstep looking for Meosha, since their scene the day before, Cam hadn't really mentioned her.

"Don't worry about her," he said seriously, keeping his eye on the television screen. "Meosha can take care of herself. We both know that."

Kalita sat back and lifted the remote to turn off the television. "You're right," she said, then clicked the television off. The lamp on the table beside the sofa was on so the room was cast in a dim glow. "I'll just go to bed. She has to come back to get the rest of her stuff so I'll just ask her what happened then."

"Yeah, you do that," Cam said, then looked at Kalita closely.

Again he noted that she was pretty. She was petite but she was stacked. He'd seen her come in from the gym yesterday and couldn't help but stare at her plump backside. Now she wore a nightshirt that had a few buttons at the top that were undone so he could see the swell of her bountiful breasts. Her legs were folded beneath her as she sat on the sofa. But she'd just unfolded them and he'd spied her smooth skin from her knees up to mid-thigh where the nightshirt stopped.

His dick was instantly alive and Cam scooted closer to her.

"Kalita?"

"Yeah," she answered, turning to face him.

"I'm not tired," he said, slowly reaching a hand out to rest on her knee. "Are you?"

Kalita cocked her head to the side, surveying him for a minute. There was no mistaking the way he was looking at her, no doubts of what he now wanted from her. Could she really do it? Her previous night's dream came flashing back, and the desire for him to touch her more intimately, to finally take her, was overwhelming.

Meosha's advice about looking out for herself rang in Kalita's ears. It was a cruel world out there, and the majority of the people in that world tended to look out for themselves. So why shouldn't she? Why shouldn't Kalita, for once in her life, do what she wanted, damn the consequences and repercussions?

Cam's hand moved over her knee, then upward to her thigh. Her body heated instantly and she closed her eyes briefly, one last bit of contemplation settling in. In her lifetime Kalita had been cheated on, she'd been used by men, cast aside by her family, and now mistrusted and wrongfully accused by her best friend for sleeping with her ex-man. Only, Kalita thought dismally, she hadn't slept with Cam.

Yet.

Opening her eyes again was like opening the door to a new chapter in her life. Kalita moved a little closer to Cam until the scent of his cologne permeated her senses.

Then she spoke with more honesty and more conviction then she ever had in her life. "No. I'm not tired at all."